AESTRANGEL

THE

CHOSEN

THE AESTRANGEL TRINITY

AESTRANGEL
THE
CHOSEN

MARIA DeVivo

4 Horsemen
Publications, Inc.

4 Horsemen
Publications, Inc.

4 Horsemen Publications, Inc.
1497 Main St. Suite 169
Dunedin, FL 34698
4horsemenpublications.com
info@4horsemenpublications.com

Cover & Typesetting by Niki Tantillo
Edited by Laura Mita

Library of Congress Control Number: 2023934356

Paperback ISBN-13: 978-1-64450-932-6
Hardcover ISBN-13: 978-1-64450-933-3
Audiobook ISBN-13: 978-1-64450-935-7
Ebook ISBN-13: 978-1-64450-934-0

DEDICATION

For JD—thank you for always planting seeds in my brain.

For SD—thank you for always encouraging those seeds to grow.

For MD—it's always for you, and always will be for you.

TABLE OF CONTENTS

PROLOGUE

Since the dawn of humans, people have created the concept of time. The rise and descent of the sun, the cyclical phases of the moon, and the change from one season to the next all serve as natural markers of time, but with the invention of the first sundial in Ancient Egypt, humankind now had a way to keep time daily.

And it was never enough, until she took over.

In the beginning, there were never enough hours in the day, not enough days in the week, never enough weeks in the year. Humans invented the notion of time, invented related words—timeliness, timely manner, timely fashion—and held themselves to standards of time, relations of time, all organized by time. It became a thing of dread and fear simply because the people forced themselves into the bubble of not having enough. The elderly lost track of time, along with their memories of it, and essentially diminished their perception of the actual length of their existence on this planet. When a person died, loved ones lamented, "It wasn't his time!" or "We didn't have enough time with her!" It was quite the pathetic corner they had painted themselves into.

To Aestrangel, the Evening Star, there was no time—no beginning, no end. She knew not the concept, was not bound by its rules, and never felt pressured by its restraints. For what is time for a demon who has crossed over all planes of existence, jumped through the very fabric of

time at will, inserted herself into human memories, and caused havoc for centuries?

And that is why it is said she alone has changed the human idea of time. The terror she has unleashed into the hearts of humankind warped their thinking, made them squirm and squeal, made them praise a short life so as to avoid the pain and suffering she could—and would—potentially inflict upon them. Little girls wore headbands made from morning glories and prayed to Aestrangel to quickly take their parents to the Underworld. And by the age of thirty, most people chose to take their own life in order to avoid the tortures of her wrath. For if she has the power to destroy the purest of angels, the horrors she can shape for the mortals is beyond comprehension.

The brutality of her existence has reigned for over 2,000 years. She has been both feared and revered by people the world over. She is The Dark One, The Enlightened One, The Dark Star, The Morning Glory. She is the one who can ravage, and warp, and bend time at will, confusing and tormenting humans in the most ugly and horrific ways. She is the all-knowing, all-seeing, and all-powerful almighty. To speak even her name is to conjure a most terrifying fate.

She is Aestrangel...

-PART I-
THE TRAINING

angel—*one of the classes of spiritual beings; a celestial attendant of God. The lowest of the nine celestial orders (seraphim, cherubim, ophanim, dominions, virtues, powers, principalities, archangels/guardian angels, angels). An attendant or guardian spirit.*

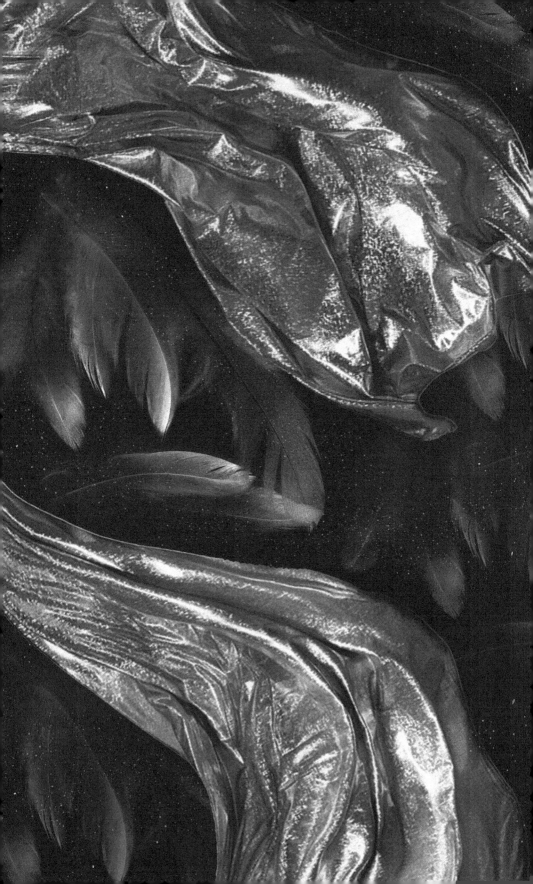

CHAPTER ONE

TIME

I'm in and out of consciousness as I descend. My body hurtles in a downward, spiral motion, and I have lost all control. There is nothing but a vast space of darkness, and occasionally bright lights flash before my eyes even when my eyes are closed. Do I even have eyes? When I open and close my eyelids, everything looks the same from the outside in. I don't know why I'm falling, how long I've been falling, where I am, or how I even got here, but when I'm able to catch a breath, or have some sort of concrete thought, I try to gather up some of the pieces, and there's one thing I am certain of...

I'm falling through time. Actual time.

My angelic senses can't even begin to perceive, or put into words, the actual construct of time, but I do know this much, it is horrible and beautiful all at once as I charge through the past, the present, and the future.

My body is pulled in all sorts of directions—up, sideways, and the most notable sensation—down. At times, I am sucked into a vortex-like maelstrom and spin uncontrollably. That's when I black out. Sometimes, I feel my essence being squeezed down to the size of a pea and shoved through the head of a sewing needle. Sometimes, my being

is gigantic, and my entire essence blankets over moons and stars and planets of thousands of galaxies. The motion is often violent and disorienting, and I sometimes have trouble even remembering who I am. I must repeat it to myself many, many times:

I am Aestra. I am an angel in the court of the Almighty Lord and Creator. I am a child of God in the purest ways. And He will be the one to save me from this.

But no one hears my plea ... because no one has come to help me. I am alone. I am in constant motion. And I am afraid. I am afraid I have been forsaken for some ungodly reason.

There are times as I'm descending that I see images—glimpses of terrifying scenes. The bright flashing lights bombard my mind with gruesome and gory sights. I see blood. Dark, red, human blood splattered on white canvasses. I see human body parts strewn across green fields. I think I even hear humans screaming in agony. When those visions come to me, I close my eyes even tighter in hopes of blocking them out. Confusion sets into my soul even deeper than before when those scenes present themselves. *Why do they appear to me? What is happening?*

I struggle to maintain some semblance of sanity—some semblance of myself—but sometimes, the harder I try, the more I can feel my memories rise from my aura and disperse into the vacuum of time, lost to me forever.

I feel a weakness where my stomach should be. There's a hollow pit gnawing its way through my essence, and the feeling of falling is shifting, changing. I'm being pulled forward, but my head is bobbing up and down in a wheelbarrow motion. My wings are heavy. My eyes are heavy. Time is speeding up and slowing down all at once. The lights flash quickly and brightly until there is nothing but a twinkling white light all around me. It overtakes me. Lulls me. I close my eyes, but it's still there. Maybe the Lord *has* heard me. I can't fight it anymore...

...I finally open my eyes and survey what is before me. I have made my way through the annals of time and am now lying on solid ground, but everything is strange. *I feel strange.* It takes me a while to get my bearings, but when I finally do, when I finally adjust to being stable, I sit up and look at this foggy world I have fallen to. There's a gray haze everywhere—a foggy gloom blankets this realm. It resembles the world of the humans, the human Earth in which I was preparing to arrive, but there is an acrid odor all around me, like something perpetually burning in the sky. I'm sitting in a field of green-gray grass, and there are dozens of small purple flowers outlining my shape where I must have landed. The flowers are humming. It's such a muffled sound that only my angel senses could pick up on it.

Angel senses.

I rotate my shoulders forward in a panic-stricken whirl. My wings are there, but they feel different. Heavier. Like something is weighing them down. It's possible they are still feeling the after-effects of my journey through time. I close my eyes and breathe in the ashy air, and panic starts to kick in... *I am not in Ilarium, and I am not fully angel.*

I bring my knees to my chest, wrap my arms around my legs, and rub the silky flesh of my upper arms. Human flesh—soft and supple just how I thought it would feel when I was to be transformed. But this is strange because I still have my wings—those heavy appendages connected to human bone. Did I disengage? Am I starting my Calling now? Didn't Camael say I would be fully human, though? Then why do I have heightened senses? Why do I still have my wings?

My body starts to rock back and forth uncontrollably, and I try to wrap my mind around what's happening. Where am I? How did I get here? Where are Camael and Revalia and...?

Lozhure.

The last thing I remember is Revalia and Lozhure taking me to The Observatory, and...

A low, growling noise reverberates through the gray valley interrupting my thoughts. At once the purple flowers stop humming and their petals shrink inward. I freeze for a moment, cocking my head to the side, tuning in to see if the noise will happen again. And it does. But this time it sounds louder, closer. It vibrates the ground below me, shaking the flowers at their stems. I don't want to stick around to see if the growl will get any closer, so I will myself to stand and move. *Go. Now. Walk.*

Unsteady, shaky legs take me across the green-gray field and up to a city street—a human city street—one that seems so familiar to me, but I can't place my finger on how or why I would know this place.

I come to the corner of a street and sit on the concrete sidewalk. I put my face in my hands and inhale. The scent of the grass fills my nostrils, and I try once again to make sense of everything. I fumble through the fuzziness that is now my memories and try to dig around

to the last thing I remember. It always goes back to the night at The Observatory. I had been preparing for my Calling, setting myself up for advancement in the Angelic Order. I was given this body—this female form—had multiple trainings with my guide, Camael, and the other Powers That Be. We were all waiting for me to have a human dream before I would be able to disengage from the temple and go down to Earth to help my human Calling. Revalia and Lozhure had both failed their first missions. Both were despondent and *apathetic*. I remember Revalia, my sweetest angel friend, and her companion Lozhure took me to that sacred temple in Ilarium. I remember I didn't want to go, but Revalia dragged me there. And I let her. There was a curious part of me that wanted to see what they were up to, but the obedient side of me fought. I remember feeling the heat of the energy source in the middle of the room and being entranced with it. I remember fighting against Lozhure as he pinned my arms to my back and pushed me in front of the Window—the place where angels observed and saw the faces of their Callings. I remember closing my eyes tight as Revalia said, *"There he is! He's so beautiful!"* And that's where it ends. I have no memory of anything after that.

Okay. This is starting to make sense. Maybe we got in trouble for trespassing in The Observatory? Maybe this is a punishment for breaking the rules? Maybe if I'm here, then Revalia and Lozhure are here, too?

I stand quickly, but the weight of my wings jerks me backward to the point where I almost fall over. I rotate my shoulders forward to straighten myself out and start walking down the streets of this odd world, searching for my angel friends. I have no clue as to where I'm going, or which direction I'm headed in. Everything looks relatively the same around here, but I can't give up. I need to find someone... anyone.

I'm unsettled as I make my way through back alleys of buildings and brick-faced houses. No matter what corner I turn, or what avenue I go down, I can't escape the fog, or the smell, or the fact that I'm alone. From the corner of my eye, I see a figure across the street, and instinctively, I call out, "Lia!" I run across the street to where the shadowy shape has gone and scream, "Lia!" again, but the figure disintegrates before I get a chance to make out exactly what it was. It vanishes like a ghost de-materializing into the thin, smoky air.

"Revalia!" I scream into the fog. "Where are you? Lozhure? Are you here? Is there anybody here?"

My voice echoes off the city buildings as tears start to swell in my eyes. "Camael? Lord? Anyone? Can anyone hear me? Is anyone there?"

I can barely see through the blurriness of the tears. The buildings look jagged and distorted behind the fog and my human eyes mist. I am crying. Tears. Angels don't cry, yet here I am—locked in this half-human, half-angelic form. *Alone.* This must be my punishment! This must be my sentence for trespassing that night! There's no other explanation for all this.

All I wanted was to do good for the Lord. My love for him is endless and boundless and knows no wrong, and if I have offended the Creator with my actions, I am truly and wholeheartedly sorry for my transgressions. I can make this right! I can make this right!

"I only wish to serve you!" I scream to the gray sky. "Forgive me, oh Lord! Forgive me and I will amend my wrongdoings, but please! Please do not forsake me! Do not abandon me in this wretched and lonely world! I will not survive without your presence! I will not be able to go on without your Eternal Light!"

I bend forward, exhausted and scared, and I put my hands on my knees. Through my tear-filled eyes, I see blood on the ground. Trails of blood in front of me, behind me, to the right and to the left, like a bleeding animal had been dragged through the streets. Fear strikes at my chest again when I realize the trail seems to be following me, and at that very moment of realization, the growling sound fills the air, paralyzing me where I stand.

I extend my wings out at full length in hopes that I will be able to use them to fly, but they are powerless here, impotent. I tuck them back in, folded at an angle so that I will be able to better ground myself to run.

And I run.

Because a giant looming presence has materialized a short distance from me, and I sense it is getting closer—gaining on me, stalking me, bringing with it a guttural snarl and a blood-stained trail.

I run through the streets, through the alleys, across the ashy landscape of desolation, back to the open field where I woke, back to the purple flowers who have now switched their humming to a deep and somber song—constantly looking over my shoulder, gauging the distance I have from the monster. But the shape in the misty fog gets closer, gains on me, and I stumble backward onto the green-gray grass as it approaches—an outline at first—a dark, hazy silhouette moves and shifts like clouds in the Earth's sky. The growls of the beast ring louder

in the air, louder in my head. I cover my ears to block out the sound, but it's no use.

I am half-paralyzed, half-ready for confrontation as I lift myself on one knee. A part of me wants to curl into an invisible ball, while another part of me is ready to face down this beast in any way I can.

It is a thing of nightmares—like a giant on two legs with gnarled horns atop its head. It's huge, with a stony exterior, like a monolith of ancient times come to life. Its eyes are cold, like gray ice, and it scratches at the ground with its cloven hooves. The purple flowers quiver in its presence, and I right myself up slowly and crack my wings out at full length.

"Leave me alone in this place!" I yell at it.

It moves a step forward, ignoring my plea. As it moves its leg, it seems to shift in shape again. It seems to shrink a little and shed its black-rock façade.

I stand my ground with a courage I didn't even know existed within me. "I said to leave me alone or I will call upon the heavenly host of angels to usher you to your ultimate salvation!" The words come out of my mouth without hesitation, but now a part of me fears my holy invocation would be useless. If I truly am being punished in this foggy world, then the legion of my brethren probably won't swoop down and save me from this damnation. Before I even realize I am doing it, my right foot takes a step backward, and I hear a chuckling growl from the shape.

It does not stop its steady, deliberate steps toward me, and as it gets closer, it changes even more—whittling down from the massive, cloven-hoofed beast who stalks me in the streets, to a shape much more different and serene. I see the shape of a man—a human man—with short black hair, stormy gray eyes, and a silver medallion swinging from his neck. He is smiling and stops a few feet in front of me. It's a charming smile, a cunning smile, a smile that could trick the most naïve of maidens to fall for his every word.

"Stop right there!" I order.

He continues to smile at me as he puts his hands up in a surrender-like pose.

My wings quiver; I can't help it. I have never been in the presence of a creature such as this, and yet somehow, I am not afraid. Anxiety, nervousness—yes. Fear? No. I crack my wings again to let it know I'm not afraid, but their weight is almost unbearable. I lose my footing and stumble for a second.

He extends his hand toward me as if to help me with my little misstep. "You can relax," he says. "I'm not going to hurt you." His voice is soft and deep, and I hear it not only in my ears but also in my chest. His voice sounds like sap slowly dripping off the bark of a tree—slow and smooth, and hypnotic.

"That's close enough," I say. "I know what you are, demon!"

He furrows his eyebrows in a pained expression as if what I had said to him was the worst thing he had ever been called in his entire unholy existence.

He takes a step closer. "Okay, okay," he says. "Fair enough."

"I said don't take another step closer or I'll..."

"You seem to know so much about what I am, but do you know what *you* are?"

I freeze for a split second. "Of course, demon!" I shout confidently. "My name is Aestra! I am an angel! Servant of the Almighty Creator of Heaven and Earth!" My voice booms through the field. Strong. Sure.

The demon smiles again at me and lets out a small chuckle.

"Ah, yes, *angel*," he says with contempt. "Have you had a look at those wings?"

I cock my head slightly to the side, puzzled. He waves a hand in my direction, urging me to look to the side at my extended wings.

I take the bait and do.

I can't catch my breath when I see the black feathers stacked up together. Black feather after black feather attached to a black quill. Attached to my back. To bone. To me! But not only are the feathers black, they are dripping with a dark substance at the bottom tips. I look to the ground and the substance is all around me. I bend forward, dip my fingers in it, bring the cold sticky substance to my face. *Blood.* I realize *I've* been the one trailing blood through the city streets.

Like lightning flashes behind my eyes, images bombard my brain. I see blood-soaked canvasses, and strewn human body parts, pools of blood against desert sand, blood-stained steel of robotic men on assembly lines. It's all too real and overwhelming, like an unbelievable dream or some long-forgotten memory. And I hear screams of terror and agony and horror and...

I fall down, rocked by the revolting pictures that catapult into my consciousness, rocked by the sight of my blackened, blood-stained wings.

The demon stands over me and extends his hand to help me up. "I am Malek," he says. "Malek Forcas. And I'm a little hurt you don't remember me. Rise, Aestrangel, and I'll explain everything."

CHAPTER TWO

HELLO AGAIN

A estrangel.

He addresses me with this strange name, yet something about that word stirs a flutter in the pit of my stomach. *Aestrangel.* Like, I've heard it before, but I can't seem to place where or when. *Aestrangel.* A strange, bastardized version of my own name—Aestra: the name given to me by my Holy Father, the Lord.

I must have a puzzled look on my face because he scrunches his nose. "Don't tell me you've forgotten your own name!" he says with surprise. "It's the name you have chosen for yourself, and that is how you wish to be addressed."

I've had enough of him—enough of this game, enough of his suave, ambiguous presence that leaves me feeling shameful and slimy. As I scramble to my feet, he steps closer to me and puts his hand on my shoulder. His touch is like hard ice clogging my insides. The coldness permeates all over my body, and I shiver before jerking my shoulder away defiantly. An overwhelming sensation invades me—*Run away from this thing!* But I can't. There's something preventing me from sprinting across this field and finding my way back to Ilarium. I feel stuck. My head is telling me to lurch forward and flee, but my legs aren't

responding, and when I look down at them, as if to yell at them to obey my command, I suddenly realize I'm naked. Normally, this isn't an issue for us angels. I was given the form of a human female to complete my mission and move up the Angelic ranks, and there was never a sense of shame or pride or the word "nakedness." Now all that is different. Not only *am* I naked, but I *feel* naked—a pained feeling radiates from the inside out. Those are human words... human emotions—words and feelings I should not have knowledge of, yet I do. In a flash, I wrap my wings to cover my body from his sight, and yell, "Don't touch me!"

He takes a step back and retreats to his "surrender" pose: palms out, hands up.

"The word you called me is not my name," I assure him. "I told you my name, demon! I am Aestra."

He puts his hands at his sides and clicks his tongue on the roof of his mouth. "Ya know, I have a name, too. Calling me 'demon' is a little offensive if you want to know the truth."

"What do demons know of truth? When you're the child of the Father of Lies, is that even possible?"

A smile blossoms on his face showing off a mouth of perfectly white, perfectly straight teeth. *Where are your fangs? Why don't you show me your true form again?* I think to myself, wondering if he can hear my thoughts. But he continues to smile, unfazed by my line of questioning. His eyes glare at me—cold eyes, like the touch of his flesh. They're gray and stormy. Dark storm clouds swirling like a hypnotic tornado, one I find so hard to look away from.

"If you're trying to talk to me using your mind," he says, "I'll have you know, those tricks don't work here."

Fog thickens around him, and his human shape seems to expand and shift with the movement of the mist. "Where exactly is *here*?" I ask.

"You don't know?"

I stare at him hard as the fog gets denser around him. It moves between his legs, up and over his shoulders, fills the empty space between us, and then engulfs me in its Sulphur-smelling waves. It stings my eyes, causing me to squint. It fills my lungs, forcing me to cover my mouth and nose and hold my breath. It's dizzying, and I am unsteady again.

"Lord!" I scream, muffled by my hand. "Please help me, Lord!"

When I finally open my eyes and adjust my vision, the demon and I are standing in the middle of a room. A strange room—one would-be retreat of a teenaged girl. There are pictures on a nightstand, a bed with purple fuzzy pillows, and some posters taped to the wall.

"What is this place? Why did you bring me here?" I demand.

"This is the place that is in your heart, Aestrangel. This is the place of your deepest wants and desires."

"No!" I protest. "That's not true! I have no idea what this place is! How can this be my deepest desire if I've never even been here before? My deepest desire is to get back to Ilarium. That is where I wish to be."

He shakes his head. "I'm sorry, Morning Glory, that's just not possible. You were cast out, Aestrangel. You're not welcome there. They don't want you anymore."

His words sting me because I fear he's right. Something bad happened. Something bad. And I know it all stems from the night in The Observatory. I look down at my blackened wings. My long blonde hair weaves in and out of the onyx feathers. Blackness. The mark of transgression. The stain of disobedience and punishment. The emblem of a fallen angel. "W...what happened?" I stammer, my voice rising in volume.

He cups his hands together and whispers words in a tongue I cannot decipher. A purple orb manifests in the space of his palms, and I see an image of Camael with Uriah and Drakonas—the other Powers That Be—huddled in a circle in deep conversation.

"Banishment."

"Absolutely not. That's ridiculous."

"But look at what she's done."

"I know. I know. It looks bad."

"But there must be a logical explanation for why she did what she did."

"...the ramifications of her actions..."

"I don't think she's strong enough to simultaneously bear the weight of humanity and the essence of her angelic nature."

"Then, with your consent, Camael, it's settled."

"There's no other alternative but to cast her out of Ilarium."

The demon folds his hands together, ceasing the transmission as I gasp out loud. "Lies!" I scream at him. I can't help but put my hands to my face and weep.

"They're not lies, Aestrangel," he says smoothly.

"Deceptions! Manipulations! Call them what you will. I don't believe you! A demon is all-knowing, and you have many tricks!"

"Look at me," he says, and I lift my head. "Look around you. Look at your wings. You can only try to trick yourself, Aestrangel. They cast you out. Bottom line."

"My disobedience to the Creator should warrant punishment, with that much I agree, but to be *here*? Tormented in Hell?"

He chuckles. "Asphodel. We call it Asphodel. Hell is such a harsh word."

"No," I say calmly, "it's Hell because the true definition of Hell is the absence of the Lord, and that is exactly what I am feeling right now."

"That's where you're wrong. The Lord is here."

"That's not my lord. I do not serve him."

The demon inhales through his nose and exhales loudly through his mouth. I think I see remnants of smoke or fog filter out from his pursed lips. "See, that's where the story gets a little shaky, dear. My Father did a wonderful favor for you. He granted you something you were burning to have."

He pauses as I raise an eyebrow. "What are you talking about?" The Morning Star? Lucifer? Did *me* a favor? I'm as confused as ever and am trying to keep it together. Demons are deceptive, and if I don't watch my every word, I'm afraid I'll fall into one of his many traps. There is no way in Ilarium I would ever seek the Dark One's advice or help. That would be one of the most blasphemous affronts to the Creator! But then again, I did something wrong. Now I need to figure out what happened after The Observatory until now.

"You can leave Asphodel, but it won't be as easy as clicking your heels together," he says.

If I can get him to reveal himself to me, his true form, his true self, and not some fog-gloom monster, maybe I will be able to better perceive the deceptions and weed out what minimal truth is buried therein. "Why don't you speak to me in your true form, demon? No tricks."

His hand moves to the medallion around his neck, and he clutches it lovingly. It's a clear, diamond-shaped pendant dangling from a silver chain. That's his *glamour*. That must be how he can mask his true demonic body. "But you wouldn't understand me, and you would be much too frightened." He extends his lower lip in a sarcastic pout.

"Of course, I would understand you!" I scoff. "I'm an angel!"

He points a long finger at my wings. "Are you sure about that?"

I pause. I look down at myself. And for the first time, I question: *What have I become?*

"You can relax those if you want," he says, waving his hand in an arch in front of me.

I don't want him to see my flesh; don't want him to see my nakedness. I don't want to be reminded of my vulnerability when I'm supposed to be facing down my sworn enemy. I shake my head.

He taps his finger against his head and then waves it at me. "No worries. Your shame is hidden from the world, Eve."

Slowly, I unwrap my wings to reveal I am clothed. A long, dark-gray tunic drapes my form, covering my body. The fabric feels alien against my skin, but for some reason, my embarrassment is immediately diminished. During my training with Camael and the other angels, I had a moment of embarrassment. I remember being called upon for something during one of our sessions, and I had been daydreaming. My face had turned hot and pink as the others stared and asked me questions. I didn't like that feeling then, and I don't like it anymore now. Even though I am covered, the mark of shame still lingers in my chest. I wonder how long it will take before it goes away fully?

"See," he continues, "you're in a kind of limbo. Like, in a holding spot, if you will. You're tainted with the mortality of the human form, with the instincts of both angel and demon. The war that rages inside of you right now is quite interesting. It's a violent combination of good, evil, and neutral. Pretty shades of white and black and grey pulling at your very soul. My Father seems to think that..."

"What did he do for me?" I interrupt. "What could I have possibly come to Lucifer for?"

He exhales. "That pesky memory again! Let's just say, he helped you. Big time. And your inability to remember is an after-effect of that favor."

I have no idea what he's talking about, so I shake my head and wave my hands in the air. "Yeah, yeah, yeah," I interrupt. "You said there was a way out of here?" That's all I care about. That's all I want. I need to get back to Ilarium and speak to Camael. I need to explain to him what happened. And most importantly, I need to beg forgiveness!

"Yes. Like I said..."

"I know, I know. The favor."

"Well, Lucifer requires you to show your gratitude."

"Gratitude?"

"Of course. Ya know, being thankful for the gift he gave you. It would also demonstrate the utmost loyalty to The Morning Star."

Now, *I* chuckle.

"The Morning Star requires you to fulfill a Calling. He has chosen you to carry out a special mission."

A Calling? For Lucifer? A mission for the first of the fallen angels? No. No. No. This can't be right. I'm supposed to have a Calling for Camael. I'm supposed to guide a human down the path of righteousness and good. That's what I've been training for. That's what I'm meant to do. How else am I to serve the Creator? My eyes go wide at the thought of being a pawn in Lucifer's army. It's ridiculous. Laughable. "And then, what happens when I complete this Calling?" I say, stifling a giggle.

He looks at me strangely as if I should know the answer to that question already.

"Enlighten me, demon. What is the result?"

"Well, you would move up the ranks of the Demonic Order, of course."

I breathe in deep, my chest puffing up under the tunic, over-exaggerating my female body, offended he would even suggest..."No! There's no way I will do his bidding! Favor or no favor! I don't even believe anything you've said to me. Let me speak to Revalia, my friend. She was with me the day we sneaked into The Observatory. She can help me explain to Camael. Please! I need to get back to Ilarium!" I scarcely notice my wings have extended at my sides. I am thrashing my arms wildly and screaming like a wild hellcat.

The demon grabs my arms, and his icy grip stops me in my undulating tracks. His cold-steel power freezes me in place, and his eyes are trained intently on mine. I see the storm in them again. The gray twister spiraling, spiraling, spiraling... It lulls me. Calms me.

"They don't want you anymore," he sings in my head. "You are not even one of them. Fulfill the Calling for my Father, and you can leave."

I note his choice of words. He said "leave," but not "return."

I pull away from him. Tears begin falling down my cheeks. "I won't do it! I won't! I can't!"

"But you've done far, far worse, Aestrangel." He stares at me—a gentle gaze. A pure and almost sweet gaze. It almost makes me feel sorry for him. He didn't choose this life. He was created much in the same way I was, albeit from different fathers with opposing intents. And while I'm scared by his words—*What have I done?*—there is a comfort in them. A strange, soothing comfort. Like I know him. Like I feel he's telling me the truth.

"Think on it, good sister. Think on it and pray. My Father is in no rush for an answer. And after what you've just been through, I'm sure you need some time to rest and figure things out. I understand it's a lot to absorb."

He raises his hand in a "goodbye" wave, and a spiral of fog rises from the wooden floor encircling him. He flashes me a bright smile behind the mist before he dissipates into thin air, but that time when he smiled, I clearly saw fangs.

CHAPTER THREE

A NEW CALLING

The demon leaves me, but not without bestowing upon me a gift. When the swirling fog subsides, I see he has left behind the purple, glowing orb. It shines brightly, illuminating the room with its violet light. That Malek is a tricky little devil, isn't he? I know exactly why he left that there—he wants me to use it in some way. Oh, demon! I will not fall for your deceptions and lies. I turn my head and try my best to ignore it, but there's a power radiating from it. A power that is so strong, I can't help but bring my gaze back to the shiny object on the floor. Ya know, I was able to see Camael and the other Dominions, maybe this is a way to communicate...

No! It's a trick, it's a trick, it's a trick! I can't be swayed by the dark one's seductions. No matter how much I want to, or how deeply I feel. The orb pulsates brighter, bringing with it a delicate hum, but like an obedient child not wanting to offend my Father, I turn my head up again and stare at the ceiling. I feel like Persephone scoffing at Hades's gifts: the kidnapped goddess stuck in the dark realm. How could Malek ever think I would...?

I need to focus my attention on other things, so I won't be drawn in by the magic of the orb. I walk around the room, trying to decipher what and where this place is and, perhaps, remember something about it. He said this place was one of my strongest wants, but how can that be? I look through the drawers of human clothing; flip through the pages of some of the books stacked upon the writing desk; examine the photographs in pretty frames on the nightstand. All are remnants of human existence. All are artifacts from a human life that once existed. Pieces of puzzles of something from long ago.

Or maybe something yet to be?

I pick up one of the picture frames and stare hard at the people featured in it. There are three women standing on a city street carrying shopping bags. The three have blonde hair, blue eyes, and bear a strong resemblance to each other. The frame itself is metal with a scroll design on the bottom that reads "Family Makes the Best of Friends." The picture gives me a chill. There is something oddly familiar about it... about this whole place. Is it possible this is where I was supposed to end up when I went on my Calling for the Creator? Could it be that that is the reason why this place was "in my heart"? Is this the manifestation of my desire to fulfill my mission for the Lord?

Or did I fail?

Malek said something about me being "tainted" with humanity. Was that some kind of hint? Did I go through with my Calling and fail? If I failed, how did it happen? Why did it happen? When Revalia failed her first mission, I remember she was so completely despondent she barely spoke to anyone, and when she did, it was somber, melancholy. It was like she was sick at heart.

And what does it even mean to have a heart anyway!

I drop the picture frame back on the nightstand and throw my body on the bed. My wings rustle under me, and I extend my arms over my head. I close my eyes and place both hands up to my chest feeling the material of the tunic, rubbing it against the flesh of my upper torso. Pulling the fabric down, I slip one hand underneath, caressing the soft, supple skin of my human body. I run my fingers over flesh, bone, breast—searching for the area where the *heart* is located. Once I find it, I relax my whole body and listen—listen for the sound of the beating from within. I count the beats, the slow and rhythmic beats, and let the slow, dull drumming vibrate through my fingers. *I have a heart!* I have body, and soul, and form, and shape, yet I have wings, and deeper perception, and can hear things in walls and in other realms, and...

"Oh, Revalia!" I call out. 'Cause if *I* can hear things, maybe *she* can hear things, too. "Revalia, please! If you can hear me, I beseech you! I implore you! I command you! Stretch out your angelic arms and find me through space and time. Save me from this Hell I am trapped in!"

The orb starts to spin on the floor. Its whirring noises force me to sit up and pay it some attention. It goes wild—pulsating, glowing, twitching back and forth so rapidly it looks like a purple blur. Could it be? Could it be Revalia calling out to me?

I can't hold out anymore. In all honesty, I can't resist, because if this is Revalia, I might be able to get to Camael and figure out a way to get back home to Ilarium.

I kneel down on the floor in front of the undulating orb and reach out my hands to it. In an instant, a magnetic field pulls it directly into my palms, and I cup my hands together the way I had seen the demon do it earlier. It's heavy yet light as a feather at the same time, and it's strong! Its power shoots up my arms in electric waves causing my whole upper body to feel tingly. "Revalia?" I say into the orb, leaning my face closer to the purple pulsating light. "Revalia? Are you there?"

A brown cloud appears in the center of it—a fuzzy image at first, but like a camera panning out of and into focus, I see it's Revalia's hair, then her face, then her body. As the scene transforms and opens, I can see Lozhure in the room in The Observatory. Revalia stands next to him while he's pinning my arms behind my back. I'm there. This is a scene from my past, and I remember it all too well.

"Ok, ok," she says to Lozhure. "That's enough. Let her go."

He releases me, and like a wild animal, I sprint for the door and leave The Observatory.

The last thing I remember about that night was going back to my dwelling. I had waited for Revalia to come home, but she never did. I remember falling asleep wondering if she was going to come back, and that was it for me. I have no other memory except my journey through time and my eventual arrival here in Asphodel, but the scene is continuing in the orb, showing me the aftermath of the events that night.

"Why did you do that?" she says to Lozhure.

He laughs. "C'mon, Lia! It was both of us. It was your idea to bring her here. It was your idea to show her."

"Yeah, but you saw how upset she got! You should have stopped."

"Hey! Hey! Don't put this on me! You weren't helpful in the 'stopping' department either."

Revalia lowers her head and nods. "I know, I know," she says in a regretful tone. "You know how I can get carried away with…" She looks and smiles brightly at him. He smiles back, but their secret moment is interrupted because both turn their heads in alarm as if they've heard something, *or someone*, approaching.

"Let's go," he says.

Revalia gives a quick nod, and they head for the door.

"One. Two. But where's Three?" a voice calls out before they can exit.

They stop dead in their tracks. "Camael!" Revalia squeaks in surprise.

He glides over to them—so gracefully, so majestically—it's like watching a school of fish in fluid motion. "Not nice," he scolds, but his reprimand is a diminutive one.

I see a pink blush rise in Revalia's cheeks. "Camael, I just…"

He waves his hand in the air and shakes his head. "The two of you. Did you really think I didn't know?"

Lozhure takes a step forward and opens his mouth to speak, but Camael stares and silences him.

"I understand. I do," he says calmly. "But what you did to Aestra…"

"I'm so sorry!" Revalia frantically interrupts.

"I know you are, child. But whatever made you think bringing her here was a good idea? Have you no sense of the weight you now inflicted upon her soul?"

Lozhure lowers his head and mumbles, "No, sir."

"Aestra is fragile, almost breakable. I fear for her. Not for her success as an angel in her Calling, but as a being of the Lord, as a servant of the Creator. She has a weakness, a deficiency, and we must all mind ourselves when dealing with her. You two… you're both something else. You've been there." He points to the Window and back to the energy source in the center of the room. "You know what it's like to change, and try, and fail. The two of you are strong—were strong going in and became stronger for your efforts. I am aware of your nightly visits here, and I allow it because you can handle it. You are embracing humanity in a very unique and rebellious way which will allow you to be more in sync with your human Callings the next time around. But Aestra…"

Wait! What did he just say? My wings start to flutter restlessly against my back, and I shake my shoulders forward to stop them, but they don't. Camael thinks I'm weak? Did he not have faith in me all along? Had he been lying to me my entire existence?

"How can I help her?" Revalia begs. "I need to make this right."

"Make amends. Mend her wounds. She hurts, and it is an alien feeling because she has never hurt before. To feel this betrayal is a good learning experience for her, and for you as well. You hurt. You fix."

"But how? What should I do?" she whines like a pathetic child. The sound of it grates on my ears.

"You know how much she adores the words of the humans—their songs, their poetry. I know she would most appreciate a poem," Camael replies.

Revalia perks up. "A poem," she repeats. "Lozhure will help me."

Camael opens his mouth, but I hear no more sound. The scene slowly fades back to the purple pulsating light of the orb.

I wish I could remember what happened after that night. I wish I had some recollection of the events that unfolded—the events that took me from *there* to *here*. For all I know, this could be one of the demon's tricks. But if it is true? If that's what really transpired after Revalia and Lozhure violated me, what does that say about Camael?

The orb starts to move again in my hands, and I focus on the purple clouds blooming within. A new scene appears—a classroom, much like the one I trained in when I was preparing for my Calling. There are many angels seated in straight-line rows, sitting straight at attention. I don't recognize any of them. Thalis and Heariah, two angels who previously trained with me, are standing in the front of the "class." They must have been successful in their missions because it appears they are conducting a training class, and only Guardian Angels can have that position.

Thalis's short hair is pinned back at the sides giving her ears an elfish look. "So, everyone," she says to the others, "after the events that transpired, we all must be mindful of the humans."

"Yes," Heariah interrupts. He moves closer to Thalis and wraps an arm around her shoulder in a comforting way. "They are the Lord's divine creation."

"But even though we have looked upon them for centuries as perfect, they are not. There is sin in them. They are covered in it. Washed in it. Born with it. And when you descend, you will have a piece of sin within you as well," Thalis asserts.

"You must remember to consult your Watcher every night. They are your guidance, your counsel—your only link to Ilarium," Heariah adds.

One angel raises her hand. Thalis points to her. "Yes, *A'don'nai?*"

"All because she loved them so?"

"Yes, that is right. When she fell, we all fell."

I close my hand over the orb to shut out the lights and the sounds. A sweeping rage rises in the pit of my stomach, and I want to scream! I know they're talking about me! I know they mean me! And what is so wrong with my love for humans? Why is my devotion and appreciation for *my* Creator's most complicated and divine creation looked upon as wrong? Surely the Lord wants His heavenly host of angels to love and inspire His precious people, His followers, His supporters, and His flock who praise His holy name in the highest of regard.

Muffled voices come through from the orb again, and I open my hands to take another peek. I'm curious as to what it will tell me this time. What other horrible things will they all say about me? It's the same scene with Camael, Uriah, and Drakonas—the one I saw with Malek a little while before.

"It's no secret Aestra has a deep affinity for the human race, and there's nothing wrong with that, but after what..." Drakonas says.

"She feels too deeply," Uriah interjects. "She empathizes with them on a higher level than I've ever seen."

"It's bizarre, you have to admit that much, Camael. It's as if she was meant to be human herself," Drakonas adds.

Camael lowers his head. "You're right," he agrees.

"Then, with your consent, Camael, it's settled," Uriah says.

"There's no other alternative but to cast her out of Ilarium," Drakonas finishes.

I feel sick. I feel sick, and lost, and abandoned, and everything in between. I'm afraid I'm going to spew up something vile from my stomach, so I move to the bed and sit down. The orb is still in my hands, the scene with the Dominions is still playing in the center, but I can't hear anything. There's a sharp ringing in my ears that fills my head with a high-pitched noise. For lack of a better word, they all perceive me as obsessed. Obsessed with the humans. My undying, unwavering love is looked upon as something villainous and treacherous. I don't under-stand. I'm at a loss for words. I am completely and utterly shocked, and empty, and alone, and lost, and betrayed, and...

A voice comes through the orb. Malek. *Demon.* I turn my so head away, so I don't have to look at him. I contemplate throwing the orb to the floor...

"Get the answers you were looking for?" he asks.

"Oh, you mean more of your lies?" I reply, and I have to wonder, who am I trying to convince? Him? Or me?

"When are you going to realize I'm not lying to you? That I will never lie to you? Hurts, doesn't it?"

I pause. "Some. But only because I don't have the full story, demon. And neither do they. See, you may not have been lying, but I'm willing to bet there was some fancy manipulation in what I saw."

He sighs and smiles. "Remember what I said, Aestrangel. If you complete a Calling for The Morning Star, you can leave. It's as simple as that."

I turn and face him in the orb. His gray eyes illuminate the sphere, canceling out all the purple light. "What if I refuse? What if I don't do it?"

"The option is always open to you. It will never be taken 'off-the-table,' so to speak."

"Fine. But in the meantime?"

"Well, let's see... you're not human. Not angel. Certainly not demon. You're something very... special. And you would have to remain in Asphodel."

I shake my head. "Until I give an answer?"

"Well, yeah. You say no one day, and the offer will present itself again the next."

"So, you're basically saying I'm stuck here. In Hell."

"Asphodel," he corrects.

I exhale through slightly parted lips. "Whatever."

"That's always been the case. I know you don't remember, but we've gone done this road before and..."

"I'm a prisoner, is what you're saying."

He shakes his head. "No! Absolutely not! That's such a nasty word."

"So let me go now."

"You can't. There's no other place for you, Aestrangel. You have no connection to any realm right now."

"Then plug in your orb-y thing and let me talk to Camael!"

"It doesn't work that way," he says. "That's not an option."

My stomach goes hollow again, like it was dropped into a nauseous wave. I'm silent for a few moments, letting the gravity of his words sink in. I belong nowhere. I am the lost child. I cannot be redeemed because there is no one to plead my case to. I have a choice in this situation. I can stay here, in Hell, *in Asphodel*. I can. I really, truly can. But to what end? If I could just get to Camael and talk things over...

"What becomes of me if I accept?" I say to him behind gritted, reluctant teeth.

"What do you want to happen, Aestrangel?" he asks coolly.

"Why do you play games with me, demon? You know good and well what I want! I want to see Camael. I want to come face-to-face with him and get answers. I need to know what happened to me."

He frowns. "Are you sure that's what you want?"

"Of course, I'm sure!"

"Then so be it. If that's what you want, if that's what you truly want in your heart, I'm sure my Father would have no problem arranging for it. Just to be clear, you agree to the deal, correct?"

I breathe in. I can't believe what I'm about to say, what I'm agreeing to do. Who would have thought that me, Aestra, an angel in service to the Almighty God, would agree to go along with one of Lucifer's schemes? But all of them in Ilarium seem to think I am a lesser angel—was a lesser angel, rather, and I really need to find out the truth. Why does Camael think so lowly of me? Why am I regarded as a... a *heretic*? I close my eyes. "Yes," I say. "I agree."

"Excellent," Malek replies, and the orb goes dark in my hands.

CHAPTER FOUR

THE ORB

The shadows shift constantly in this gloomy, strange world. As I walk along the side streets, I see figures and shapes from the corners of my eyes, but I know there is nothing there—not really. What I see are merely figments of my imagination, images conjured up in the deepest parts of my psyche, fragments of not wanting to be alone. If this world is what Malek truly said it was—the wants and desires of my soul—then I really am alone, abandoned here.

This form of Hell is all mine—mine to bear alone. It's personal, like something tapped into my subconscious and formed an elaborate cage fit for my fears. I dare not to think of what other people must endure! What torments and tortures await them in their personal Hells? In Ilarium, there is peace and love and the ever-dominating presence of the Creator. There is warmth and color and music, and my heart swells at the thought of my home! But here? Malek calls this place Asphodel. I know the word. It is a word of the ancients. A word attributed to plants and neutrality. *Asphodel.* The word sounds so much prettier than *Hell,* but at the end of the day, they both mean the same thing: the absence of God.

For as long as I can remember, I've been told the story of The Morning Star. Lucifer. The Light Bearer. He Who so Loved the Lord. I was taught the cautionary tale of how jealousy flooded Lucifer's heart at the dawn of humankind, and how he sought to overthrow the Creator in his supremacy. Father is said not to play favorites among his children, but there was something divinely special between Him and Lucifer. Because even as a Guardian Angel, Lucifer had high-ranking powers and was kept close in the Creator's court. When the Lord created humans and showered His love and divinity on them, Lucifer felt lost—abandoned by Him. And no matter how hard Lucifer tried, the jealousy steadily increased, but the Lord continued to show His love and forgiveness to Lucifer, no matter how much he rebelled. And even when it all came to a head, when Lucifer had finally crossed the line and fell, the Creator left His proverbial door open, hoping one day Lucifer would beg forgiveness and return to Ilarium.

After all The Morning Star has done to upset the balance of things, after all his tricks and schemes, and lies and deceptions, wars, and pestilences, Father still loves him and still yearns for him to come back. If that isn't the greatest testament to the unwavering love and devotion of the Creator, I don't know what is! And maybe—just maybe—there's hope for me still! There is no way in Asphodel that whatever transgressions I have taken part in come close to the atrocities of He Who Holds the Lightning Rod. The Lord must still have love and forgiveness for me too. He must want me to return home just as much as He longs for the redemption of Lucifer!

My word is my bond, and I have agreed to go on a Calling for The Morning Star. But I have the best of intentions. I fear that if I don't at least give it a shot, I will never escape this fog-gloom world. I fear that the Powers That Be have no access to this time and space in Asphodel— they cannot hear my calls for help, my cries of sorrow, and my pleas for an audience with the Almighty. I can only wonder what his assignment will entail. A Calling in Ilarium has one motive—help a human. Guide them on the path of righteousness and lead them down the road of good. I suspect Lucifer's mission will most likely be just the opposite. *What will he make me do?*

I am scared. A deal like this can certainly bring nothing but devastation, and I don't want to hurt anyone. Yet, I fear that is exactly as I will be told—lead a human down the path of evil and guide them on the road of destruction. This is wrong. The ends do not justify the means, I know

that! And I can't go through with this! I can't defy the Lord any more than I already have. I open my mouth to call out to Malek. The words "I can't" make their way from my lips at the exact moment I see them.

Them.

Hideous shapes and creatures lurk in the shadows, shifting in the wind. They're not Malek. His true form was much different. More tangible. More real. These shapes are something else. I squint my eyes to see them clearer, and I nearly lose my breath when they come into focus. Faceless beings bound in heavy silver chains. Ogres with eyes and mouths sewn shut. Beasts with hunched-over backs and exposed spinal cords. Nightmarish giants clobber their ghoulish bodies throughout the city streets. I close my eyes and hope when I open them again, they will be gone. But they're still there. And when I open my eyes to look at them a little longer, I realize—this is *their* town. This is *their* home. My physical presence has merely invaded their space.

I close my eyes and repeat over and over: *Be not afraid, I go before you always. Come follow Me, and I will give you rest.*

I open my eyes again to see them dissipate back into the mist. I am alone here, but I am not alone here. This is the place where anger, resentment, and guilt live. This is their home. *I'm* the monster to them— the black-winged fallen human-shape. They are just as much afraid of me as I am of them, and if I stay here in Asphodel any longer, I will surely succumb to the madness of it all. This is what my entire existence would be like—running from the monsters from within, and it is going to drive me insane. I, too, will transform among the fog, and I shudder to think what form I would take.

My wings crack open and fold out against my back, and I take off at a sprint to return to the building with the familiar room. *My room. My dwelling. My place.* The black feathers rustle wildly against the wind, and I am weightless as I dash through the city. I extend my arm and open my palm, trying to catch the fog with my fingers. I run. I race. I glide. I move on instinct because my eyes are shut tight, and I imagine I can fly. In my mind, a flock of black birds encircles me, raises me up, lifts me off the ground, and elevates me to the highest point in Ilarium where I come face-to-face with the Lord. *And he will raise you up on eagle's wings...*

I look to my left, and there they are! A handful of black birds are hovering at my palm. Of course, not the flock from my daydream, but they are right there, right in my grasp. I stop running and keep my palm turned upward. The birds slow down, flittering in a circle around my hand. I swipe my right hand in front of them to shoo them away, and in an instant, they are gone. Vanished. *How did they...?*

Not angel. Not human. Not demon. I have no place. I belong nowhere. But I have power unknown—power untapped.

On a hunch, I bring my hands together, fingers barely touching. As if on instinct, I move my hands back and forth, as if I am rubbing the empty space between my palms together. It feels like a magnet, like it's pulsating. There's a power there that's growing stronger and stronger, and I must pull my hands apart a little at a time to make room for the essence that's building in strength. Fog swirls into the space as my hands separate about a foot apart. I think of the beautiful music of Ilarium—the voices of my angel kin singing their sweet hymns in majestic choirs. Voices that produce song and instrument at once in sounds no human ear could ever detect. Immediately, in the space between my hands, in that glorious magnetic field of power, a wooden box materializes. Its ancient-looking lid creaks open, and I hear their sound—I hear their song! Oh sweet brethren of Ilarium, sing to me like only you can! The song lifts me, fills me, reminds me of my heavenly origins, and it brings me right back down to the reality that is my current state of existence. I clamp my fingers shut, making two balled fists, which breaks the energy between my hands and causes the music box to cut off its song and disappear.

What is this power I have just discovered? And does Malek know of this? When I was angel, I didn't have the capability to will objects into temporary being. This is something different. Something strange. Something I must surely keep to myself for now. This little revelation also has me wondering, *What else am I capable of doing?*

Once I get back to the brick façade building, I go straight to the room, leaving the birds, music box, and fog monsters behind me. The moment Malek brought me here, it fascinated me, but I hadn't had a chance to look around and investigate. I guess now is the time to fulfill my curiosity. There's a small opening at the bottom of the nightstand next to the bed, like a mini-bookcase. I sit down on the floor and start looking through the books within. Poetry. Oh, how I love the human words! How they mesh and mingle and dance together to create beautiful scenes. Poetry is musical—it's the music of the spoken word and it makes me swoon. I look through book after book—Shakespeare, Longfellow, Hughes, Frost, Dickinson—and the words weave, twist,

create, inspire, dream. I am taken away by the beauty of it all—the agony, the despair, the wonder, the hope. The human lexicon is teeming with all sorts of words. It breathes with every syllable, comes alive with every synonym, and denotes a myriad of emotions. Human language is unlike anything in Ilarium. We have words and speak, but there is no concrete language of the angels and...

As I open a book with Poe's name on the spine, a yellowed piece of paper falls into my lap. I reach down and pick it up. The paper makes a crinkling sound in my hand, and as I examine it, I can tell it's incredibly old. Carefully and delicately, I unfold the creases. Handwritten at the top of the page is the word "Aestrangel."

Aestrangel.

I continue to read:

Great angel-winged arms
Pluck the dusk from my eyes.
She appears to me like a dream—
White light fantasy,
Chrome rust memory.
Hidden secrets of the morning dew
Form on my brow.
I know not their meaning.

How strange, and yet, so hauntingly beautiful. I read the poem three more times—to absorb, understand, and connect. I have never heard this poem before, nor is there any author listed on the page, yet I am drawn to it. It feels like a secret, like some far-off mystery from some far-off realm. And there's that name—the name that Malek calls me—Aestrangel. He says I sought that name out for myself, that I assigned it to myself. I don't think I am the author of this poem because I know I would have remembered writing such enigmatic words. It could very well be that I read this poem at some point, fell in love with it, and because the title is so closely related to my name, perhaps that's how I adopted it.

Aestra.

Aestrangel. Aestra angel? A strange angel? An estranged angel?

Did I write this poem? Is it about me? Was it written for me? Am I the great angel-winged arms? Am I the girl in the dream? Am I Aestrangel?

I fold the paper back up and return it to the Poe book. Then I put all the books back the way I found them and sit on the bed. Every moment I stay in Asphodel, I become increasingly confused. When I think I've figured out one puzzle, I realize I've opened a different section on the board. I've said it before, and I'll say it again... if I could just speak to Camael! He would be honest and forthcoming with me. He would help me through this dark and confusing time. He would save me! If I just had Malek's orb, maybe I could...

Wait.

I don't need Malek's orb.

If this world is my deepest heart's desire, and I can create tangible manifestations of my wants, then I don't need Malek's orb because I can make my own.

I cross my legs on the bed and straighten my spine at attention. My wings are folded over each other across my back in their usual resting position, but as soon as I cup my hands together, the feathers start to quiver. I close my eyes, imagining a mist-like sphere appearing from my palms. Swirling, pulsating, mirroring the magnetic feeling of the one Malek had. I think it up. Dream it up. Will it up. And it rises—smoke-like at first but taking shape as a brownish-gray ball with violent storm clouds deep within.

"Camael," I whisper into it. "Camael. Where are you, my guide? I need you, Camael. Please! I am lost and alone without you. I have been trying to..."

The clouds in my orb rotate and flicker. "Please," I beg of it. "Show me Camael." And as if on command, I see him. He's in The Observatory with Revalia and Lozhure. The glow from the energy source illuminates the room, washes over their faces in a glittery light. They look like ancient angelic statues with stoic faces. Revalia and Lozhure's wings are fully extended—their feather-tips touching in an angel embrace, but they are holding hands in the most basic of human gestures.

"Speak to me! Please!" I cry, and immediately, their voices resonate in my room.

"This is unprecedented," Camael says to the two of them. "And you will need to proceed with the utmost of caution."

They both nod their heads reverently, their eyes fixated on the ground. Revalia squeezes Lozhure's hand tighter.

"This Calling is the only one that the two of you can carry out together, and you must be on the same page in this mission."

Revalia and Lozhure are getting ready to disengage for a new Calling, one that requires the two of them to be together. This appears to be some kind of private training because there aren't any other angels

around. I've never heard of this happening, nor has it been something we were taught from the proverbial history books. When Camael says this is unprecedented, he really means it!

Yet, I'm not surprised to see this. Revalia and Lozhure had both failed in their first rounds, separately. The two of them share a special bond—a very *human*-like bond. In a way, it seems sort of natural for them to be working collaboratively on a Calling.

"What if we fail again?" Revalia whispers. She sounds so fragile and weak; I can barely hear her.

Lozhure looks sharply and raises his eyebrows at her.

Camael gently unfolds his wings to brush against Revalia's shoulder. "Think of it not," he says soothingly. "You two are well suited for this. I wouldn't have it any other way." He smiles, and her eyes change from brown to blue as she smiles back at him.

Lozhure folds his wings and lets go of Revalia's hand. "Lozhure?" Camael asks, "Why the hesitation? Speak to me, child."

Lozhure rocks his body nervously back and forth and stares deep into the well of the energy source, but from my vantage point, it's as if his eyes are trained directly on me. He fidgets with his hands, rubbing his fingers together. He seems distracted, almost in a trance.

Taking a chance, a stab in the dark, I whisper "Lozhure" into the orb. He flinches, cocking his head to the side as if trying to pick up on some other-worldly sounds. Did he hear me? Is it possible that...

"It's ok," Revalia says, petting his arm. "Camael believes we'll be ok."

"Do you believe that? Do you think we're ready for this?" he asks her quietly as Camael looks on.

"I do," she tries to assure him, or maybe herself.

"Lozhure," I whisper again, and he stares back into the well, back into my eyes. I doubt he can see me, but I know he heard me that time.

Camael's face darkens. He takes a quick step toward Lozhure, puts his hand on his shoulder, and spins him around, away from the light of the energy source. "What happened? What's going on?" he says frantically.

"I... I don't know," Lozhure stammers, coming out of his trance.

And it occurs to me—Camael lost contact with Lozhure for that moment. Camael couldn't tap into Lozhure's thoughts because something else was invading his essence. Camael couldn't read Lozhure because something else was inserting itself into Lozhure's consciousness... *me*!

I fold my hands together, collapsing my orb, and Camael, Revalia, and Lozhure vanish in a puff of gray smoke. The last image I see is of Camael's shadowy face. He looks unnerved, worried.

But I'm not. I think I may have figured out a way to solve my problem of being stuck in Asphodel. While Revalia and Lozhure are getting ready for a new Calling, I have a little window of time to contact Ilarium. It's not much, but it's something!

CHAPTER FIVE

CONTACT

A dark, winged shape hovers in the distance against a golden horizon. The sun is melting off the side of the Earth, casting shadows on the green terrain. The figure flies closer into view. It happens in slow motion, yet the movements are jagged and jumpy. A mass of black hair covers the face of the figure, disguising the identity of the dark presence. Rust-colored wings extend like mechanical arms barely moving, barely flitting. Yet the figure flies toward me. As it draws closer, I realize the color of the wings is more than some reflective trick from the setting sun. The feathers are not really feathers—they are hundreds upon hundreds of razor blades stained in blood. Old blood caked on them like brown metal decay. New blood, still bright and red, drips from the razors' edges and saturates the green field below. I stand in the field, huddled behind a large oak tree, praying to stay out of the path of this dark and twisted creature—the angel with strange wings.

I hear voices behind me and turn my head to see who is there. A group of four humans huddle together in a circle, cowering at the approaching being. I hear their moans of agony—their cries of their impending fate. They pray to the apparition to spare their lives. Beg the creature to have mercy on their souls.

The angel lengthens her body so that she takes on the image of a deadly missile. Her legs and wings are horizontally behind her, and she dips her head *low to allow herself the momentum to charge at the pack of humans clustered together. She gains speed and descends faster than my eyes can pick up on and circles them twice before shooting back into the sky like a rocket. A collective gasp of relief rises from the group, and I too, relax my tense muscles and sigh for them.*

But it was all too soon as the angel made her way back to them, charging faster than she had before, the speed of her body a blur to my sight. She extends one wing to her side, rounds the group a final time, and takes off into the purple twilight.

In an instant, my face is covered in a warm, sticky liquid. I look down at my hands, and my entire body is splattered in their blood. The moans and groans from the group have ceased, and in its place, I hear the squishing sounds of body parts toppling over each other and onto the blood-stained grass. Entrails steam up in the early evening air as the four human bodies have violently turned to eight. All is silent. Desolate. Void. Until...

"Enjoy your sleep?" a voice says over me.

I open my eyes and strain to see who is speaking, disoriented from the dream and the reality.

It suddenly hits me that I had a dream! This was the moment Camael had been waiting for—the moment I had been waiting for. An angel must have a dream before they can go on their Calling, and that was the last step I needed to have before I could be dispatched. However, I'm not in Ilarium, and those wicked visions I experienced in slumber felt too real to be just a dream.

I must have passed out on the bed after I had turned the orb off. I had felt tired and weak, and I had promised myself I would close my eyes for a few minutes, and... well, I guess I must have been out for a lot longer than that because my arm is stretched over my head, and my hand feels like pins and needles throbbing against the flesh. I sit and shake my hand out, and Malek takes a seat at the edge of the bed. It makes me uncomfortable to know he can waltz in and out of here whenever he pleases, and I wonder if he knows what I discovered about my power here in Asphodel. I can't mention anything to him about it yet, or ever for that matter. And now that he is here with me, I'm not sure if I'll be able to make contact with Revalia or Lozhure today like I had hoped.

"Dreamless," I lie, rubbing at my eyes with my balled-up hands.

"Nothing at all?" he pries.

I shake my head, not wanting to tell him about the images. Not wanting to relive that ghastly scene.

"That's usually the case," he says. "Dreams keep our minds in overdrive when what we really need is mindless rest. You'll find that you won't dream much while you're here. You might never ever experience one."

"That's not so odd, ya know. We didn't dream in Ilarium."

"Yes. Typical. Dreaming is a human thing, I suppose. Just another funny joke your creator used on his children." His hand brushes against my calf as he changes his position, so I curl my knees to my chest, trying to create some extra distance between us.

"Joke?" I say, resting my chin against my knees.

He answers me with a devilish grin. There's something so charming and handsome about it. Our eyes meet, and as I stare into the gray depths of them, the violent storm does not appear. Rather, there is an ocean—deep and wide—and gray waves gently lick at the brown, sandy shore. It is calming, and I find myself relaxing my body, leaning forward to better hear his words—to be closer to his attractive façade.

"What do you know of your father?" he asks.

My face twists quizzically. "What do you mean? In what sense?"

"I mean, what do you know about your maker? What's his story? His origin? What makes him tick?"

I think on this for a second, and the pre-programmed answer flies from my mouth. "He is everything. Infinity. Eternity. He was always here. She will always be here. They transcend time and space."

He chuckles. "Yes, that is all well and good, but what's his *story*? Everyone has one. It's what shapes us, motivates us, makes us who we are."

"I'm not quite sure what you mean about a *story*. How can *God* have a story? He has no beginning and no end. There! There's your story. Alpha and Omega. Period."

He claps his hands together, and the sound is like thunder in the room. "Lesson One!" he proclaims. "You are exactly right! How can he have a tale to tell when he is the almighty force in the entire universe? But think about this, Aestrangel, how is that fair? How is that fair to all the puppets he controls on his multitude of strings?"

"Fair?"

"Precisely. It's not. Your creator has no concept of struggle, of... of..." his voice trails off, unable to find the word he's looking for.

"You have nothing to say because you're pulling at straws," I taunt. "When you talk about things being fair, you speak of nonsense. The Creator creates. That's what He does. And if He is the source of all creation, then we are to obey Him, cherish Him, and love Him for the loving parent He is."

"I want to tell you a story," Malek says calmly. "An important one, in fact. Then maybe you'll understand a little bit better." He waves his hand in the air and the room transforms. Everything melts away into an inky black void of nothing. Slowly, like lights being turned on systematically, stars begin to fill the sky. We are both suspended in an illusion of space. I feel weightless, like I'm hovering in the void, but I am cognizant enough to know this is a mirage. "If there is no beginning and no end, we can say that this just was, or is," he says looking at the vast space around him. "Do we agree on that much?"

I nod.

"How old are you?" he asks me.

"I know no time," I respond.

"But you are not as old as your maker, correct?"

"Correct."

"And there are ones that came before you, but not as old as your creator. Correct?"

"Yes. Because time is a farce. It's a figment of measurement. It's a..."

"Human concept," he interrupts.

I nod again.

"At some point," he continues, "your creator found its breath and fashioned companions for himself. He called them *Angelos* and designed them to be his messengers, his confidantes. He loved them all the same, yet differently in his own way. And while he refused to show any of them any ounce of favoritism, there was no denying the bond between the creator and The Morning Star. There was a strong and powerful love between the two, and it was said Lucifer's existence was revered as the most precious creation of all. Fashioned from the purest light in the center of the cosmos, Lucifer was your maker's most holy friend, and his rise to the head of the heavenly host was immediate from the time of his design."

He reaches for my hands, and I reluctantly place my palms in his. They are ice, and I shiver at first touch. With all his might, he swings me around in this gravity-free environment, and we both go spinning out of control. Stars whir past me, like streaks of light flashing in front

of my face. It reminds me of my journey through time before I came to be in Asphodel—how I twisted and turned and fell through the pipes and spigots of time.

When we stop, we are in a green landscape of open fields—a lush and vibrant garden teeming with trees and flowers and plants of all kinds. The crisp air almost makes me believe we are actually standing in the midst of this pristine countryside, but there is an underlying scent of Sulphur, and I know we are still in Malek's homemade movie.

"Yet, your creator decided he wanted a little bit more. So, he played. He experimented, if you will. He created universe after universe, planet after planet, life form after life form, until he at last settled on his ultimate design... Earth." Malek spreads his arms open and gestures around us. We are in Paradise. The Garden of Eden.

"And he marveled at every little sub-creation that grew. And multiplied. And flourished. He used the Earth to create all types of life, and before long, those forms of life gave way to other forms of life in a domino-effect reaction. But that still wasn't enough. He still wasn't satisfied. From the earth—the fertile soil, the dark-gray clay, and the brown, fragmented dust—he fashioned a man, Adam, and a woman..."

"Eve," I say completing his sentence.

"Lilith," he corrects.

I raise my eyebrows suspiciously. "What are you talking about?" I know not the name, heard not the tale.

"Have I lied to you yet?" he asks as he points across the meadow. In the distance, under an oak tree, I see them—Adam and Lilith. They are perfect human forms with long black hair. Their caramel skin glistens with a shiny newness that practically eats the shadows cast by the large tree.

"Your god wished for them to flourish, too. They were his new creations, and he loved them so. But in this new love of his, his attentions shifted. No longer did he hold court with his angels. No longer did he require them to sing to him—something they had all looked forward to doing each day and night. Things changed. He changed. His priorities changed as he delighted in his latest invention. Lucifer took note of the change, and for the first time, resentment wiggled its way into the heart of the Angelos.

"Then time was created and moved forward. Your maker realized Adam and Lilith were not happy. They worshipped him and gave praise to him, but together, they were not a good match. They quarreled constantly and disagreed on mostly everything. Lilith had desires separate from Adam. She wanted to create, invent, explore, and most of all, not be subservient to him. Adam had other ideas, of course."

I watch their figures in the distance, and their angry faces indicate a fight. Lilith turns on her heels, her long, black hair leaving its scent behind her.

"She left him?"

Malek nods. "At the far edge of the garden, there was a cave by a sandy beach. She walked there alone so she could be *alone*." He snaps his fingers, and instantly, I hear the ocean roaring. Sand crunches between my toes as Malek and I stand in front of the gray cave. I know this place—this beach, this ocean—this is the place Malek showed me in his eyes a few moments ago.

"And what became of her?" I ask.

"Well, your creator was obviously upset. This was not what he had intended for his people. What's the saying? Go forth and multiply? How could his new friends multiply if they were living separate lives? So, he needed to intervene. And who best to send, but his messengers, his Angelos. Your beloved Camael was a lowly angel at the time, and your sacred creator felt this would be an effective way for him to prove his worth and loyalty and move up the ranks of the Angelic Order. But nothing like this had ever been done before, and your creator was fearful of Camael's transition to the human world. And so, it came to be that your maker sent Camael, accompanied by Lucifer, to Earth in order to help a human—to put her on the path of 'good' and 'righteousness.'"

"A Calling," I whisper.

"The very first one of its kind."

I see two robed figures entering the cave: Camael and Lucifer. Malek grabs my hand again and walks me over to the entrance so that we can witness the action. I can't hear their voices, but by their facial expressions and body gestures, it is obvious Camael pleads desperately with the woman to return to Adam. Lilith's face is steadfast, and she closes her eyes and turns her head from him. Yet every now and then, during their silent conversation, I notice a look, a glance, a very palpable gaze that happens between Lilith and Lucifer. Camael's arms are wild in his begging, and the look of frustration on his face is damn-near pathetic. Every plea, every request, every demand Camael makes of her is met with opposition—a stomping foot, or a closed-eye head bob, or a frantic shake of her head. In between this back-and-forth, there is nothing but

a mere smirk from Lucifer's face, and a hint of admiration in Lilith's eyes when she catches Lucifer's stare.

"Does she...?" I begin.

Malek sighs deeply. "Ah, yes," he breathes. "You could say it was like love at first sight. The Morning Star was drawn to her instantly. I mean, just look at her! Her beauty alone could make any being—celestial or human—fall madly in love. But it wasn't just that for Lucifer. It was Lilith's spirit... her *defiance*. Yes, she loved and worshipped her god— she did and always would—but she felt like she was being forced into a situation that she didn't like. Simply put, she didn't like Adam. In fact, she detested him! And she was making a choice. She would rather live alone than with him. End of discussion."

"Free will," I insert, and Malek nods.

"Lucifer was enamored by her willingness to take her situation into her own hands. She was using the gifts she was given to fashion her own destiny."

"But that was not the destiny the Lord had intended for her."

"Exactly."

I continue to watch the scene. Camael looks frustrated beyond belief because Lilith is obviously not budging! Lucifer puts his hand on Camael's shoulder and whispers into his ear, and almost immediately, Camael hangs his head low and exits the cave.

"What's happening now?" I ask.

"Isn't it apparent?" Malek responds.

"Wait! Did Lucifer send Camael away? Did Camael *fail* his Calling?"

Malek snickers. "Yes, Aestrangel. Not only did your precious and perfect Camael fail his first Calling, but he failed *the* first Calling ever devised!"

My wings quiver against my back, and I try to control the rustling, but I can't get them to calm down. Maybe because my anger has turned up a notch? A part of me still distrusts Malek, but a part of me kind of believes him. What reason would he have to lie to me, other than to convince me to do something for Lucifer? Which, by the way, I've already agreed to, so what would be the purpose of a lie at this juncture? I've already committed. He doesn't need to convince me further. Unless the sole purpose here is to *show* me *the truth*. The *real* truth. The legends and stories that have been hidden from angelic eyes and ears for eons, like dirty little secrets.

"What gives him the right?" I lash out before I even get to analyze what I'm going to say. "What gives Camael the right to pass judgment on *anyone* if he's nothing but a failure himself?"

"Starting to see my point?" Malek says.

I suck in my anger, restraining myself from further lashing out. I've said too much, let too much emotion show. "Don't get too ahead of yourself," I say. "But I will admit this is a very interesting tale."

"There's more. Would you like to hear it?"

I swallow hard. "Please do."

"Lucifer stayed with Lilith after he sent Camael back to Ilarium, under the pretense he would work hard to convince her to go back to Adam. But Lucifer knew good and well that was not his true intent. Every day that passed, he grew more attached to Lilith. His affections strengthened, and she too, fell deeply in love with him. She called him Samael, meaning tempter and seducer, for the name Lucifer was too intense and magnanimous for the human mind to interpret and repeat. 'I shall call you Samael,' she said to him with a loving smile, 'because you are the venom of God sent here to poison me with your kisses.'"

In the scene before me, Lucifer and Lilith embrace and passionately kiss. Something stirs inside me, like an awakening. I know the word "passion," and I even know *how* the emotion is supposed to be felt. But to be in its presence is like nothing I've experienced. Their passion for each other suffocates me like the air in the cave has been ignited. It takes my breath away and forces me to gasp.

"For forty days and forty nights, Lucifer, under the guise of Samael, stayed with his Lilith, the first woman to ever walk the Earth. His love for her was beyond compare, and at times, he felt it might even surpass the love he felt for his creator."

"So, why did he leave her?" I ask.

"Well, the human mind can be tapped into much easier than the mind of a high-ranking angel. Lilith had a dream one night, and in that dream, her god had called Lucifer back home, demanding he return to Ilarium at once. Lilith, being the obedient servant she was, insisted Samael do as he was told. So, he did. And when he returned to his home, he was met with the wrath of God like never before. His creator forbade him from ever returning to Earth and from ever interacting with or seeing Lilith again. And as this was taking place, Camael was dispatched once again to Lilith, this time with the orders of doling out her punishment."

"The first punishment," I say as I see Camael enter the cave again. Lilith is weary, tired. She's hunched over, carrying a bundle in her arms, and her eyes are puffy and red as she continuously weeps for the return of her Samael.

"Lilith's punishment was Camael's redemption, so to speak. As an unsuitable wife for Adam, she had no place in the world. Camael banished her to the cave—she was forbidden to ever leave or attempt to go back to the garden."

"That was her punishment? But isn't that what she wanted, anyway?"

"Yes, at first. But Lucifer changed all that. As did the child she bore from their union."

My eyes go wide. "A child? Lucifer and Lilith had a child together?" I say in disbelief.

"The one thing that kept Lilith holding on. The one thing that gave her the will to live in Samael's absence. But when Camael came with god's punishment, he took that away from her. You see, Aestrangel, Camael declared that not only was Lilith banished from the garden and made to stay in the cave, but even worse, for every living child she would bear, her next one hundred would have to die." Malek points to the image. The figure of Camael touches the bundle in Lilith's hands, and after a moment, she falls to her knees in hysterics.

I feel sick to my stomach. Nauseous. "Oh my god," I respond because, honestly, I don't know what else to say.

"You said it, alright. And remember, that's *your* god, not mine."

"And all this happened before Lucifer fell? Before he rebelled against the Lord and took his unholy throne?"

"Oh yes," he says, grabbing for my hands. "That's next on the agenda." And with that, he spins me around in a macabre-like dance. The oceanside landscape disappears, and we are back in the great expanse of the cosmos.

THE LOVE SONG OF LILITH

"You know all this, do you not?" Malek asks as we dangle, hand in hand, in the manufactured heavens.

I nod my head. "I know about The Fall."

He clicks his tongue against the roof of his mouth. "Such a shame. And kinda not fair, don't you think? Would be nice if they would school you in what really happened. Ah, yes, but that would jeopardize your big man's entire operation, wouldn't it? Can't have his angels feel *sorry* for The Morning Star, now can he? 'Cause that pesky little caveat—ya know, *free will*—would most definitely put a wrench in any of his plans."

"You're wrong," I say, but in my heart, even I am unsure of my response.

"So tell me what you know about The Fall," he presses.

"Lucifer was the one that was so loved by the Creator until human-kind came into existence. The Morning Star gave everything to the Creator but felt ignored at the dawn of the human race. Over time, he resented the Lord and grew jealous of His people. Lucifer committed the ultimate affront to the Creator and the entire Angelic Order when he renounced the Lord and set out to overthrow Him. The story of Lucifer is the example by which we live, or rather, how *not* to live."

He shakes his head and huffs, "He was most loved by the Creator. There is some truth to that. At one time, Lucifer was the most revered, but your god's love is fickle, and once something new came along... your answer is so clear cut, so very *textbook*. Didn't you think to question your teachings? Didn't you ever think to stop and ask why? Or were you so blindly willing to accept everything they presented to you as holy gospel?"

The smirk on his face is too much for me to take. I lower my head and stare at the open space beneath me. I feel so stupid and embarrassed because the way he puts it in front of me makes me sound ridiculous. Am I stupid for thinking they want me back in Ilarium? Have I been an idiot for having belief, faith, and *trust?*

From the corner of my eye, I see Malek moving his hands. My eyes are still looking down, and suddenly, the ground rushes to meet my feet. We're back on "land." Back in the Garden of Eden. "I'm sorry if I made you feel bad about yourself," he says as he approaches me and touches my shoulder. "I want you to understand completely and fully. The Morning Star has been portrayed as the bad guy for so long, and your father has always been represented as the good. I want you to see there is no bad or good. It's all a matter of perception."

"Or in your case, *de*ception?"

"You still hold on to your deep-seated beliefs," he says in defeat. "I don't know how many times I have to tell you..."

"I know. I get it. You haven't lied to me. So, get on with it. Tell me the rest of your story."

He sits down on the grass and pats a spot to his left, welcoming me to sit next to him. "Okay," he begins after I tuck in my wings and sit pretzel-style on the grass. "Lesson Two. The Morning Star was devastated by his separation from Lilith. He was even more horrified by the terms of her punishment. And that is when he decided he needed to take control over his own destiny."

"Revenge? Lucifer renounced the Lord because he wanted to get back at Him?"

"It's a bit more complicated than that, Aestrangel. Yes, there was a bit of revenge in there—along with jealousy and feelings of abandonment—but at the core of the matter, at the true heart of it all, Lucifer wanted freedom. He had the power of free will, and he was determined to live his life away from the shackles of his master."

"But it doesn't add up," I say. "Why not just leave? Why rebel? Why amass an army of angels and storm into the Lord's realm demanding he abdicate his throne? See, this is where the affront to the Lord plays the largest role here. Because I can feel sympathetic for his lost love, and his anger, and his loneliness and abandonment, but to wage war against your Father? That is unforgivable."

"Wage war? Again, a pre-programmed answer. It wasn't as calculated or as brutal as you think it was. Alright, alright, the thought of power and supremacy is, of course, seductive. And yes, Lucifer did have plans for taking over the heavens. But he had the best of intentions, I assure you. After what happened to Lilith, he couldn't stand living under his creator's regime, and if he were to take the helm, he would have done things very differently."

"But he didn't."

"He *couldn't*. Because after all the jealousy, after all the feelings of resentment, Lucifer still loved him, and ultimately, he decided to leave on his own terms."

"Free will."

"Surely there was fighting, anger, and fire and brimstone, but think about it... this was the first time *anyone* had stood up to your god. In a way, The Morning Star is a pioneer... a hero!"

I raise my eyebrows at him and stifle a laugh.

He smiles. "What? Too much?"

I hold my thumb and forefinger about an inch apart. "Just a little," I say and a small snicker escapes my lips. I clamp my hand over my mouth like a naughty child saying his first naughty word.

Malek laughs back. "I'm glad you're relaxed a little because in a few moments..." his voice trails and he points out into the distance of the open field. "Don't get scared, okay? You know this..."

"Isn't really happening?"

"Precisely. But it's going to feel real to you. Especially *you*, ya know, with your non-angel, non-demon self."

I inhale. There's nothing funny about what he said that time.

"Right about now," he says, still pointing. Off in the distance, the sky quickly darkens like night rolling in, taking the day prisoner. The wind starts to howl, a hellish cacophony of screams and wails from unknown sources. One of the black clouds begins to swirl, and in its twisting motion, it opens a hole in the center of itself. Malek moves closer to me and wraps his arms around my shoulders. "Hold on," he shouts over

the storm. My wings tense up as his upper torso brushes against the feathers. Out of the cloud, a thick bolt of purple lightning charges to the Earth, splitting the ground wide-open with a thunderous *crack* and igniting a massive fire in the forest around us. The ground beneath us quakes so violently, I am shaken off balance and practically wind up in Malek's lap. "He felt like lightning piercing the Earth's core," he screams as he stands. "Come on, we need to get out of here!"

I scramble to my feet, and Malek waves his hand in the air. He's brought us back to the cave where Lilith lived, but it looks different, darker. And there's a somber aura in the air—a sort of sadness, a yearning. Everything is gray. The seas have risen, and a brown, mossy substance has grown over the cave rocks.

"Is Lilith even alive?" I ask.

"Oh, yes! There was no death for humans in the beginning."

"Why are we back here? What was all that before?"

"When The Morning Star fell, the Earth changed. Almost like a hammer splitting open a coconut. The seas rose, vicious storms raged across the landscape, and everything was in total disarray. Lucifer broke through the barrier of the world and transcended."

"Don't you mean *descended*?" I ask.

"Eh. Again, all about perception. Remember, for us immortals, there is..."

"No space and time," I finish for him.

"And with the absence of his creator, Lucifer was able to transform— to *become*. The transformation was something even your god couldn't have predicted. Lucifer was able to shape himself in *his own* image and likeness by fully embracing the power of his free will.

"After all of that, he searched for Lilith. He had not forgotten about her and wanted to fix whatever wrongs were done to her. He traveled the ends of the Earth searching, and when he finally reached her, she was still in her cave—alone.

"When she saw him, it was like time had stopped for her. She recognized him immediately and called out, 'Samael! My Samael!' From the moment Lucifer left her to the moment of his return, Lilith had done nothing but wait and survive. And you could imagine what went through his mind when he saw the remains of his deceased child laying neatly on her rock table. Blanched bones positioned in the outline of a small baby."

I imagine the scene, and I flinch in horror. "Had she gone mad?"

"Well," he says as we enter the cave, "that is up for debate. I personally think any form of love is a mild form of madness."

"You would, wouldn't you," I say, rolling my eyes.

The inside of the cave is in shambles, exactly how Malek described—a place set up only for survival. I can't believe she stayed like that for so long. I can't believe she waited endlessly—never knowing if her love would return to her, never knowing if the next day would be "the time." I feel sorry for Lilith—the human woman so enamored with the angel. She sacrificed her entire existence for the chance to be with the one she so loved.

I watch them—Samael and Lilith. I watch as she falls helplessly into his open arms. She tucks one arm under his and grabs on tightly to his shoulder, caressing the feathers attached to the jutted-out bone. With the other hand, she smooths her palm across his face, her fingers dancing over all his lines and creases. Her face dims briefly when she touches his forehead and feels the sharp, bony fragments of his horns, but she ignores it and continues to inspect him, to feel him, to *remember* him. He clutches her hands and takes a step back so he, too, can be bathed in her presence. He smiles at her, for she must be exactly as he remembered. She smiles back, and her cheeks get hot and red—a blush of embarrassment? Passion? Both?

"'You came back,' Lilith said," Malek relays what I cannot hear. "'I'll stay if you'll have me,' Lucifer responded."

"Be with me always," I hear a woman's voice say. Lilith's voice. Not in the cave, not from her image, but in my head. I heard it plain as day. The voice was sweet and gentle, but it startles me.

Malek cocks his head to the side. "Did you hear something?" he asks.

I nod.

"You heard Lilith speak?" The volume of his voice raises a little in an aggravated tone.

"I... I think so," I stammer, unsure.

"Hmmm," he huffs. "That's interesting."

In the scene, Lilith falls to her knees before Lucifer. Her long black hair fans out at his feet and across the stony floor of the cave like an onyx carpet. He leans forward and rubs her back in a circular motion. Her body twitches from his touch as she rotates her arms, adjusting to the thin bones sprouting from her shoulder blades. They grow wild, vine-like, and inch by inch, they fill in with luscious raven-colored

feathers. *He gave her wings so they could be together.* When her transformation is complete, she rises, and they embrace.

I shake my back to the side and glance at my own black wings. The obsidian feathers gleam with a pearlescent finish, and if I tilt my arms the right way, I catch a glimpse of a rainbow of colors sitting on top of the deep blackness. These are my gifts from Lucifer. Much like the ones he bestowed upon his beloved Lilith.

"My parents do make a lovely couple, don't they?" Malek says.

"Your parents? You are the child of Lucifer and Lilith?"

He laughs. "How did you think demons were created, Aestrangel?"

"But how can that be? Camael destroyed their child."

"Their first child. Then ninety-nine more after that. Tragic, but my mother has fashioned a glorious throne for herself from the backs of her dead children. See, the punishment of Lilith can never be reversed, so she must endure one hundred deaths of her children before she can raise a live one."

Before I get a chance to respond, Malek snaps his fingers, bringing us back to the Garden. It has been left unscathed by Lucifer's Fall. Adam is there, accompanied by another woman—one with pale white skin and long blonde hair.

Eve.

Malek begins walking toward them at a brisk pace, and I trot behind, still piecing things together. "But the other angels? What about them? The others that fell after The Morning Star?" I say to his back.

"They fell for the love of human women," he sighs, "the descendants of Adam and Eve. Yes, well, after my Father renounced god and all that—I wasn't kidding when I said he was like a pioneer!—others began to take control of *their* own destinies, and the rest is history. See, Aestrangel, there are two types of demons—The Old Ones, *Apokomistai*, and The New Ones, *Nekudaimones*. The Old Ones are the original ones, the ones from your heavens who dissented. The New Ones are those, like me, who were created in some way—whether it be The Morning Star breathing his breath into a tar pit or from the union of Samael and Lilith."

"And me? Where do I fit in in all of this?" I ask.

Malek stops in his tracks and turns to me. "I don't know yet. And that's the absolute truth."

We stare at each other for a moment, and I get lost in his eyes. The beach is quiet there, and the sun is setting in the distance. Sunlight from the Garden glints off his medallion, and I have to squint to keep his gaze. I am drawn to him, drawn into him. My insides are being pulled forward as if they need to jump into his eyes and swim in the deepest part of his ocean. I sigh, breaking our trance. If I only knew what happened to me, then maybe I could let myself drown in his eyes forever... "Why can't you just tell me what happened?" I ask, exasperated.

"I just did, Aestrangel. Were you not paying attention?"

I huff at his sarcasm. "No! That's not what I meant. Why can't you tell me what happened to *me*? What *I* did. Why *I'm* here. All that. You seem to know so much about everything else."

"Because I can't. That story is not mine to tell. I probably couldn't even if I tried. You asked my Father to make you forget. That's on you, Aestrangel. That was part of your deal with him."

"I... I *requested* to forget?" I stammer in disbelief. "Why on Earth would I ever do something like that?"

"I've learned that beings of all kinds can do crazy things when there's so much at stake. But, right now, you need to focus on *your* promise to my Father. What do you know of Adam and Eve?"

I put my hands on my hips and flare out my wings. "Eve was created from Adam's rib. One and the same, yet different. The temptation of Eve brought sin into the world for the humans, for which they needed to be cleansed and forgiven."

He opens his eyes wide in mock surprise. "Wow!" he jests. "Camael must have been so proud of you. You have everything memorized!"

I ruffle my feathers in annoyance and tap my foot on the grass. "Do you plan on going anywhere with this?"

"Lesson Three is all about Eve. When Lucifer realized Adam had a new partner, his plan began to take form. The infamous forbidden fruit was created by your god as a tool, a device, to keep the two humans in check. Your maker couldn't risk another Lilith situation, so he exuded a little more control over the two. But my Father, the smooth talker he is, knew Eve would be easily tempted. Who knows? Some say my Father had an unfair advantage, but that's beside the point. Lucifer knew the one tragic flaw of the humans, and he exploited it in such a grand fashion that sin and death were now words that would be commonplace among his creator's most grand design. And why not? He had to witness and suffer through the death of one hundred children, and what? The others are free to reproduce as freely and as happily as they please?"

"What's the tragic flaw? What's the one thing humans have that is their ultimate undoing?"

"Words. The ability to speak and write. Language. Language is their ultimate downfall. It is the one necessary gift for the advancement of the race, and the one thing that can be altered and manipulated to do the Devil's work."

CHAPTER SEVEN

THE BOOK OF MALEK

I truly feel the pressure of my dilemma pounding against my temples. It's such a strange feeling—being torn between these two opposite worlds. I am an angel, dammit! A vessel of the Lord. His messenger. The manifestation of his love. Yet, I am nothing. A shadow. A concubine being prepared for evil. I know this is wrong. I know all of this is wrong. Just entertaining a conversation with this demon before me is against everything I was taught and believe—this demon who appears to me in his human guise as a clever and handsome young man with jet-black hair and stormy gray eyes. His physical appearance alone is enough to tempt even the strongest-willed woman.

But here I am.

Conversing.

Entertaining.

Plotting.

"You don't use actual words in Ilarium, do you?" he asks me.

I shake my head.

"Did you ever wonder why?"

"We don't need them. It's not like that," I answer. "We're not exactly corporeal, and things work a little bit differently there."

He raises his eyebrows in a menacing arch, and his eyes glitter with a sparkly gray hue. A smirk forms on the right side of his mouth. It's at this very moment I understand the appeal of his temptation because there's a twinge in my stomach. Not one of sickness, or anger, but something unfamiliar to me. Admiration? Attraction?

Malek waves his arm in the air in a circular motion, and we are transported into a human simulation. "The humans are so far removed from their creator, in all aspects of time and space. The separation often causes them to be somewhat gullible and naïve. And because of their disconnection from grace, they become open to words. *Susceptible* to their power."

We're sitting on a bench in a crowded subway train car, but the scent in the air lets me know this isn't real—we're still in Asphodel, and this is another movie in Malek's catalog. The people here are packed shoulder to shoulder like sardines in a flimsy tin can. Their faces are drawn and weary with stress and depression. There is no joy here. No happiness. Not even a spark of contentment. All that is here is a vacancy—an absence of harmony, an absence of the Lord.

Malek sits in between me and a young man. He has shaggy brown hair hanging low in his eyes, and his cheeks are sunken in a bit underneath his eyes. He scowls as he stares at the people in the train car. His presence makes me uncomfortable, and I question why Malek chose to sit here.

Malek turns his head to me. "The beauty of life is the power of free will. It is the greatest and most destructive attribute of any human being. And the ultimate human goal is to be happy, right? But at what cost?" He nods his head to a man standing to the left of us holding on to the handgrip of the train. The motion of the subway car jostles his wallet out from his shallow coat pocket and onto the floor at the feet of the young man sitting next to Malek. The young man's eyes quickly dart to the overstuffed leather wallet at his feet, and he reaches down, almost instinctively, to pick it up. His eyes are wide with wonder and confusion as he examines the wallet.

Malek puts his palm out in a "stop" gesture, and everything around us pauses. "See here," he says. "There are two ways in which this could play out. The young man can keep the wallet and reap the financial rewards of its contents. Or he can return it and get some sort of chivalrous satisfaction for doing the right thing."

I study the man's frozen face. "He'll give it back," I say. "Most humans would rather be morally fulfilled."

"You are so sure about that? You don't really know his situation or anything about his lifestyle. You don't know if he's hurting or struggling. Maybe he could really use that money. Humans will do whatever it takes for that one supreme moment of joy. It doesn't matter to them if that moment lasts a lifetime or is a passing breeze. They want it. They need it. They *have* to have it. And you see, that's where I come in. The desire for a moment of ecstasy is so powerful, the need alone so overwhelming, that when I swoop in, it's all too easy. All it takes is a tiny little push, a simple suggestion, to propel them in the right direction."

"Don't you mean 'wrong' direction?"

"Again, my dear, that's a matter of..."

"I know. *Perception.*"

"I knew you were a quick learner," he says flashing his perfectly white teeth. "Look at his face. Look at his eyes. There's a sadness in them. A hint of desperation, almost. He *knows* giving the wallet back is the *right* thing to do, but he wrestles against what he *wants* to do. Or should I say, what's right for *him* to do in this situation. So, I intervene. Make things a little clearer for him. Make his decision a little *easier.*"

Malek snaps his fingers, and we're back in "real-time." The train car moves again, and the young man stares wide-eyed at the wallet in his hands. I must admit, I can understand how this would be tempting for a human—money practically spills out from the folds of the case. Malek turns his head to the man. "Whoa!" he exclaims, his voice altered to one I don't recognize. "Looks like your lucky day, bro!"

The young man's face beams. He nods his head at Malek and then quickly slips the wallet into his pocket.

I punch Malek's arm and frantically scream-whisper to him, "Wait! That's bogus! You totally manipulated him!"

"Did I?" he says from the corner of his mouth. "Or did I use words to validate what he was already feeling?"

I shake my head. "No," I sigh. "That's evil. It's demented. It's... it's... *wrong!*"

"But is it really?" he says, and the train comes to a stop. "Let's find out. Let's see what he does from here."

The train begins to empty out at the waypoint, and the young man rises to get off. He lovingly pats the thick wallet in his pocket. Malek stands, pulling me with him. Behind a sea of people, we follow him

through the turnstile, through the corridors, up the steps, and out onto the city street. The sun blinds my eyes as I emerge from the darkened tunnels, and I am overwhelmed by the sounds and smells of the bustling city. It's as if there is a separate life-force here—a distinct rhythm and heartbeat and oxygen supply. It makes me dizzy—off-balanced. Malek grabs my hand to not lose me (or his mark) to the crowd. "C'mon," he says, dragging me toward him. "Let's see where our guy goes." He points his forefinger in the direction of the young man, and time seems to speed up like we are on a fast-forward track. We're amid the people, but we're not. We're in the middle of time and space—outsiders looking in—and everything whirs by us in streaks of jagged lights. The only countenance that I can clearly distinguish is the young man we are following.

We watch him go into a flower shop and use money from the wallet to purchase an enormous, colorful bouquet. Then he uses some money to purchase a bus ticket, and we finally speed the clock to see him arrive at a hospital. An old, frail woman sits in her hospital bed. She's attached to wires and machines, and the air smells of her impending death, but when the young man trots in and presents her with the flowers, her face lights up, and for a moment, she forgets where she is.

"His mother will die tonight," Malek says as we shift to the country road. The sky has changed to a black, inky canvass. It's much quieter here. A forest surrounds us on either side of the overpass, and there are very few streetlights illuminating the way. "She'll die, but the memory of seeing her son and her favorite flowers will be a comforting memory as she transitions worlds. In this case, I'd say the ends justify the means."

"I do understand. Truly, I do. But you're leaving out the other side of the act. What about the man whose wallet was taken? What about him? What are the ramifications on his life? His family?"

Malek smiles. "Does that even matter? A man with that much money in one place surely will be okay. What I showed you had some real value. Depth. There's no monetary equivalent to that."

I frown at his convenient response because I know there's a reaction to every action. And yes, while the young man who stole the wallet ended up using the money to do something good—something he probably wouldn't have had the means to do otherwise—there are still long-lasting ripples for the other people involved. I can't even be sure if Malek knew what the intentions of the young man were, for he certainly could have taken that money and easily have used it for something bad. "Then, show me the man," I say.

He runs his hand through his hair. "I can't."

"Why?" I press. "Because it doesn't 'work that way'?"

"No, Aestrangel, it doesn't. That moment in time has passed, and I am only privy to the images I directly influence."

"Now what does this mean for you? Was that your Calling or something? Are you set to 'move up the ranks'?" I mock him. I'm agitated. Even I can hear the sassiness in my voice. I want to rattle him, throw him off guard, and make him feel less confident—less cocky. I want him to squirm a little bit and let *him* know that *I* know what he's up to.

"Not a Calling. Just a little maintenance work. Lucifer's constant presence in the world needs to be fulfilled in some way or another." He pauses as a car goes careening past us and slams into a guardrail about one hundred feet from us. "Your turn," he says pointing at the wreckage.

I gasp as smoke pours from the hood of the car. The driver manages to roll her window down, and she screams for help. Malek taps me on the shoulder, and I look behind me. Another woman comes jogging. She's wearing a tracksuit and headphones, and I assume she's out for her nightly run. Malek raises his hand to pause the scene like he did before.

"There are two options here, right?" he says. "The jogger could help the woman in the car, or she could jog along her merry way."

My heart pounds, and I can actually hear the thumps and thuds in my ears. "No!" I yell. "You're wrong. No one has to die here tonight. The jogger could simply call for help. No one has to get hurt."

"Look at that car, Aestrangel!" he pleads with me. "That smoke will soon turn to fire, and that fire will soon turn very ugly. By the time anyone gets here, the driver will already have perished."

I look back and forth between the jogger and the wreckage. The jogger's face has a look of horror and shock. The driver of the car's head and upper body barely hangs out of the car window. She grimaces in pain, unable to remove her seat belt and crawl out to safety. Her door must be jammed too. And I stop to wonder—when Malek stops time, is the woman still suffering? Is she still feeling the pain of the crash coursing through her body? Is she still in fear?

"What do you think the jogger will do?"

"What any person would do! She'll help the driver! This is a bad accident that can be salvaged. She would want to help her."

"Yes. Most human instincts drive people to help. To preserve other human life. To save. But this time, I want you to tell the jogger to walk away," he says casually. "Look at her face. The thought has crossed her mind to help, but she's scared. It's so extremely dangerous."

I walk closer to the jogger, the statue of a woman, and I study her face. Even as she stands before me frozen in time, Malek is right. Her hesitation is obvious. One foot is set forward, toward the wreckage, but her upper body is tense and slightly twisted to the side as if she were ready to run away. And then I stare into her green eyes. Her eyes are pleading—as if to say *Why me? Why does it have to be me to help?* I take a step behind the jogger and look over her shoulder at Malek. "This is a test, right? My preparation? My training?"

"Quick learner," he says before snapping his fingers and bringing the scene back to life.

Flames begin pouring from the hood of the car, and the driver starts to scream even louder. "Please!" she cries to the jogger. "The door is stuck, and I can't get my belt off. I think I broke my leg! Please! Help me!"

I swallow hard as the jogger takes a step toward the car. In a split second, I try to rationalize all the possibilities of preventing the jogger from helping the driver, much like the string of outcomes that came with the man and the wallet.

Why would Malek ask this of me if there wasn't something larger at play here?

I put my hand on the jogger's shoulder, stopping her in her tracks. She turns her head, startled that I'm there. Her green eyes look even more scared and confused as she tries to rationalize who I am or how I got there. I freeze, not knowing what to say. Normally, I would be the champion, and tell her I would rush right on in by her side to help that driver. But now, I'm going to buck against my natural inclinations, and I find it a daunting task.

Tell her to walk away, Malek's words play in my head, and I try to formulate some kind of response or excuse. My fingers start to tingle as I press them harder into the woman's shoulder. "Hey! Do you have a phone? Call the police or something! That car looks bad. That's dangerous!"

The woman pauses and thinks for a second. I can see the struggle in her eyes. It fascinates me, as I've always assumed in times of need and ultimate despair, humans would pull through and allow their instincts to shine the light of good. I'm perplexed, mesmerized, and at the same time, I'm questioning everything I thought I knew about the Lord's divine creation. She's trembling before me, all because of a simple suggestion I injected into her mind. I did that! That was my power asserting itself! My wings flutter behind me, sending sparks of ecstasy up my spine. The sensation fills me, makes me feel light-headed, like a wobbling of inebriation. And, yes, I can tell the jogger wants to give assistance in the most basic and humanly possible ways, but she also wants no part of the wreck and so desperately wants to run away. She fights with her decision for a moment, her eyes darting back and forth over mine, searching for a way out—searching for an answer.

When she makes her decision, she nods in agreement at me and turns her back from the accident. As she reaches into her pocket and pulls out her phone to dial 911, the car explodes, and we both fall to our knees covering our heads. Malek runs over to me and helps me up, and we run along the trail into the forest.

I'm shaking. Out of breath. "The driver! She... she... *died*!"

"But the jogger didn't. You saved her life. She has three little boys at home who would have been without a mom. Sometimes, what is deemed as an act of selfishness is beneficial in the long run. Sometimes the individual must put themselves first for their *own* greater good. These random acts of intervention should be the proof you need to feel confident in your Calling for my Father."

This is something I had never considered before, but now, I understand Malek's point of view. The Calling I have to complete for Lucifer may have negative implications at first, but it seems maybe the different strings of outcomes aren't necessarily going to be diabolical. "You're saying that what I'll have to do for Lucifer is along the lines of this?"

Malek nods. "Undoubtedly."

He takes us back to the room—*my* room—and I sit down on the bed. I'm exhausted and much is weighing on my mind.

"I'm going to go for now, Aestrangel, but I'll be back soon."

I don't answer. I close my eyes and wave a dismissive hand.

"Let me ask you one question?" he says.

I lift my head.

"You felt it, didn't you? That rush. That intoxication."

I keep my head steady and my eyes closed, but I can see him smiling. He's smiling because he thinks he won.

"That's the reward for doing something right, Aestrangel. And you can feel that way always if you choose. Are you ready for this?"

I lie my face down on my pillow and speak out from the side of my mouth. My words are muffled, but I know he's heard me quite clearly: "Let's do this. Let's do it and get it over with."

-PART II-
THE CALLING

strange—*unusual, extraordinary, odd. Estranged, as a result of being outside of one's natural environment. Foreign. Outside of one's previous experiences. Odd. Queer. Unaccustomed to or inexperienced in; unacquainted. Weird.*

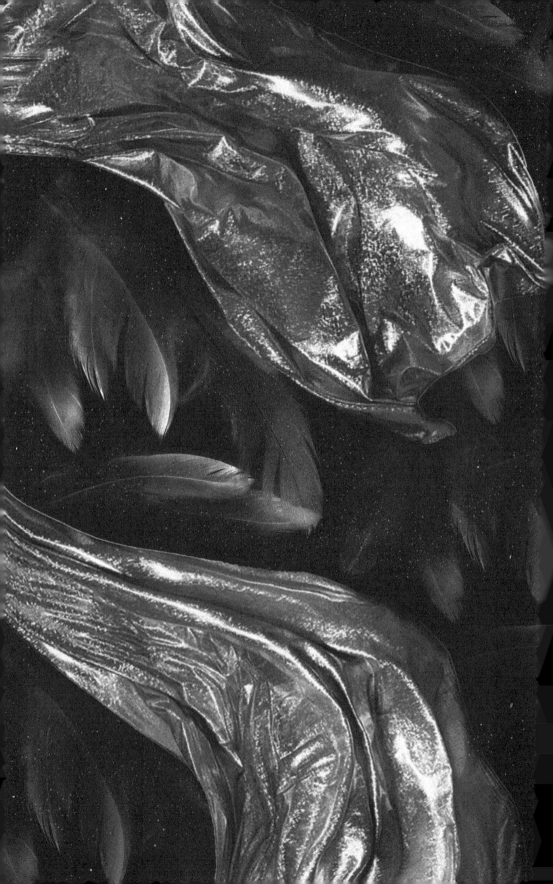

CHAPTER EIGHT

A NEW TRAINING

I'm most certain Malek will soon be summoning me to begin my Calling, and I understand there's not much time left to get out of this arrangement. I wish I had more time to play with the power I have discovered. To think of all the wonders I could create using the power of my imagination! Oh, but I will have enough time for all that if I fail, or back out at the last moment, because there's no denying the facts, and there's really no other way to describe it—I am trapped in this world because I belong nowhere. I belong Now and Here—in this particular moment, in this particular place. Asphodel. The ultimate Nowhere.

As a last-ditch effort, I create another orb in the negative space between my hands and command it to show me Ilarium. In my heart, I wish to see either Revalia or Camael, and sure enough, I am blessed with the image of Revalia and Lozhure. The sky is dark around them as they sit in a field of yellow and white flowers. Lozhure's legs are extended, and he props himself on his hands behind his back. Revalia lies with her head in Lozhure's lap and her knees tucked to her chest. His right wing pulses a baby blue color as it gently caresses the shape of her curled body. They look peaceful, serene. But there's an expression of worry and concern on their faces.

"I hope we're doing the right thing," she says to him.

His feathers sharply change to a dark navy blue before relaxing to the soft color, and he grumbles under his breath, not giving her the satisfaction of a response. He looks annoyed with her, with whatever situation they've gotten themselves into.

Her eyes turn up to look at him. "I know you don't want to hear it, but..."

"Lia, we've been through this a thousand times..."

"Now it's a thousand and one," she says as she sits on her knees and comes face-to-face with him. "I just don't want to mess this one up, ya know?"

He sighs heavily. "I know. I've always known. I know how important this is to you."

She smiles, wraps her arms around his neck, and fans her purple wings open with a hard cracking sound. Her wings have obstructed my view of them, and I try twisting and turning the orb around to get a better vantage point, but it's no use.

"This is the most important Calling I'll ever have to complete," she says. "And I wouldn't want to go on it with anyone else but you."

The image of them in the orb is starting to fade away, and something on the inside tells me Malek is approaching. In desperation, I scream into the ball, "Lia! Lia! You have to help me! I'm here! I'm in Asphodel!"

Revalia's wings stiffen for a split second, and then she retracts them onto her back. Her head cocks to the side and she says, "Did you hear something?"

Lozhure perks up, too. His brow is furrowed and he looks nervously around—the expression much like the one he made when I called out to him the other day.

Revalia stands and turns her face to the sky. "It kinda sounded like..."

"Revalia!" I scream again, and her whole body seems to shudder.

She heard me!

"That...that can't be..." Lozhure stutters.

"Aestra?" Revalia whispers, low at first. "Aestra?" she repeats, raising her voice. "Aestra!" she screams to the open sky a third time. She's worried about me; I can hear it in her voice. There's a real fear there that makes me unsettled. If I could only reach out to her, let her know where I am, maybe, maybe she can tell Camael, and they would send the cavalry.

"Lia!" I scream back. "Help me, Lia!"

Lozhure scrambles to his feet and grabs Revalia's hand. "Lozhure!" she says frantically. "It's Aestra! I know you heard it! I know you did!"

He nods his head fervently. "But... but...I don't see how it could be Aestra. Maybe it's an illusion or something. Maybe it's an echo passing through Ilarium."

She's panicking. She lets go of Lozhure's hand and starts walking in circles in the field, her eyes trained on the sky above. She's looking for something. Searching.

"Leeeeee-aaaahhh!" I yell again.

"She needs help, Lozhure!" Revalia cries. "I can hear it in her voice! She needs me!"

Lozhure grabs her hand again and jerks them downward, forcing her to look at him. "It can't be Aestra. You know that. She's weak. She could never punch through time and space like that. No. Wherever she is, she's far away from here, and her weakness couldn't even wish to reach us. Not here. Not anywhere."

I stiffen at his words. How dare he say those things about me? I think about what Camael had said, and I remember his implication that he too, believes in my lack of strength, my lack of... of... power! I steady my wings behind me and breathe deeply. Surely, Lia will come to my defense and...

"I know," she whispers to Lozhure as she lowers her head in shame.

Heat rises in my chest, and my wings start to flutter uncontrollably *She knows? She knows? What on earth does she* know?

"Her frailty could never manage, could never link her back to Ilarium. I just..."

Frailty? The one being in this universe who I thought would be on my side is now saying I'm weak?

She continues to speak to Lozhure, but I can't hear what she says. The image fades a little bit more and the sound has been muted. I hear a clicking sound from down the hallway like thick nails tapping on stone, so I quickly close my hands together, dissolving the orb and making Revalia disappear from me yet again, and leaving me stranded once more.

Nope. There is no cavalry coming for me or *my soul.*

My head starts to pound, and I am out of breath, like someone punched me in the soft spot on my belly, knocking the wind out of me. How could they all turn against me like that? What did I do to make

them deem me weak? I'm not weak! I've ventured through space and time ... and *survived*! I'm trapped in a Hell dimension and have not gone completely insane! I'm taking charge of my own destiny, on my own terms, by my own hand! And they call that *weak*? Frail. Feeble. Ineffective. Useless. That's what I am to them! Well, if that's how they feel, then I'll be certain to prove them wrong!

I pick up a picture frame from the nightstand, and in a moment of pure anger, I throw it clear across the room. The glass shatters into a hundred tiny shards as the door to the room opens wide. I catch a glimpse of stony black hooves before they transform into the feet of a human man. Malek had gotten his medallion around his neck, making his identity change to the one I am accustomed to.

"It's just about show time," he says with a grin.

I stand and rub my hands together, trying to erase any last remnants of magic from me. "I'm still a little confused, ya know," I say. "I don't understand how you expect me to succeed in this mission when I have no idea what I'm going to be doing. You really haven't given me any proper training, either."

"You don't need any training, Aestrangel. I gave you history. Knowledge. That's all you really need."

"No!" I yell at him. "What about the transformation? What about taking a human form? Infused memories? A Watcher?"

He stares at me blankly. These are all concepts he knows nothing about. When I was trained by Camael to fulfill my Calling, it was an arduous process. Angels would be sent to Earth in the form of a human, an actual human. We would have a family and memories, and because we would lose our wings, our humanness would often be one filled with trauma and pain. The only connection we would have to Ilarium was through our Watcher—the Nephilim—the offspring of the humans and fallen angels. But I guess none of that means anything to Malek because he stares at me like I have nine heads.

"There's no transformation," he says after a moment. "No Watcher. No guidance needed. That's how much The Morning Star trusts his family. We don't need babysitters, Aestrangel. We don't need fake memories or a lesson in the 'human struggle.'"

"Well, I was taught we would have to *be* human in order to adjust to the human condition, and we would be infused with human memories, a story..."

He licks his lips. "You mean lies?"

"A *background*," I snap, correcting him. "A background to blend in with them. It allows us to experience their pains and joys."

"So, let me get this straight. Your creator wants to see his children suffer? Rip off your wings, put you in a mortal shell, and let you feel the very cells in your strange body die all over you. That doesn't sound nice to me. Doesn't sound kind and loving. Kinda sounds like he enjoys watching you suffer."

I want to smack the smirk right off his face! When he says things like that, he disgusts me beyond belief! "No greatness is ever achieved without some degree of sacrifice," I say with finality, but he's triggered something in me. The way he puts it makes me think *Are we playthings for the Almighty?*

He chuckles and reaches into his pocket. From it, he pulls out a long, black box and walks over to me. "This is what you *will* need," he says, opening it.

Inside, there's a necklace. It's like the one he wears. A long silver chain with a dark purple crystal attached. "A medallion?" I mock, batting my eyes and placing my hand over my heart. "For me? Why, you shouldn't have!"

"You'll need to wear this or keep it on you at all times."

"To hide my wings?"

"Yeah, and..." he motions to the side of his forehead, right underneath the hairline. He gives me a strange look and motions for me to do the same. I take my hand and mimic his actions, smoothing my fingers and palm across the surface of my nose, up to my forehead, and over to the right side where my flesh meets hair. A sinking feeling overwhelms my stomach when my fingers probe at a protruding nodule on my head. It's about three inches wide and three inches raised. I dart my hand to the left side, and to my surprise, there's another nodule rising from my flesh.

Fear grips me from within, tightening my chest and making it hard for me to breathe. "Hor..." I start to say.

"Horns," he says, vocalizing my fear.

A dizzying wave rocks me off balance, but Malek doesn't miss a step. "The medallion will take care of all that." He takes the necklace out of the box, quickly walks behind me, and slips it over my head, fastening the clasp in the back. Instantly, I am calmed, like a warm blanket descended over my body and soul, outside and in. I look down at the purple crystal resting between my breasts and can feel it throbbing on

my skin, pulsing with power right in time with the beating of my heart. I am electrified and lulled at the same time. Heavy and light, as if I can walk on air, but I am fully aware of the gravitational pull forcing my legs to be grounded. It's a strange feeling, for sure.

Malek stands next to me and throws his arm around my shoulder. "We look good, don't we, sis?" he says.

He stands about a foot taller than me, and I turn my head to look at his face. His skin is smooth and flawless, like a living, breathing statue. Up close, it glistens with a preternatural sheen—a devilish shine to hide the monster within. He waves his free hand into the air and an ornate mirror materializes before us.

I can do that too, ya know.

And here we are. Malek and me. Arm in arm. Two beasts glamoured by some strange magic. I study us both—smooth skin, gray eyes, black hair. I barely recognize myself in this guise, but it oddly feels natural. I am a vision of perfection—a goddess brought to life and set in a human form. I touch my supple cheeks, feel the outline of my chin, run my fingers through my long raven locks. I can't help but smile at our reflection because we are too flawless not to. Malek smiles back at me in the mirror. "I take it you approve?" he asks.

I'm speechless. Dumbfounded. I break from his arm-hold and walk closer to the mirror, admiring myself—my shape, my form. I twist and turn to the side, taking in the vision of my human body, my perfected self. My hair nearly reaches the floor, and I heave it over one shoulder as I continue to make faces at myself and smile. I bend forward to look deeply into my new gray eyes. And just like Malek, I see it—a violent storm brewing in the pupils. It looms on the horizon of my eyes, dark clouds slowly churning in anger and rage. I blink my eyes quickly to break my trance for I fear I could get lost in them forever. My attention turns back to my beauty in the mirror, and I realize it is the spitting image of Malek—the female version of the strikingly handsome demon. It's no wonder the humans get lost in him and his exotic looks. I can't even imagine how they will react to... "It's that I never thought..." But I stop and turn to him. Malek and I look alike. We are the male and female versions of the same dynamic force—the same *demonic* force— forged together by some of the strongest magics imaginable. I look at him, at myself, and back to him before I pull back for a second and ask, "Did you call me 'sis'?"

His face darkens, and he frowns at me. "No one ever helped me in my Calling, but I'm gonna take a guess you don't remember any of that." He's being serious. His tone has shifted a bit. Do I detect a hint of jealousy in his voice? "But if that is how Lucifer wants it, then so be it. Seems he has hand-chosen you for something great, and I, being the obedient child I am, have agreed to assist you in your task." He drags me back to him, and we face the mirror together. "Say hello to Malek and Aestra Forcas," he says, squeezing my arm playfully. "Twin brother and sister who have turned twenty-one and are out seeking fun and adventure. We're looking for the ultimate thrill of a lifetime! And that's what we'll get in Arizona when we sign up for The Wild West Tours. Two weeks of camping, hiking, rafting..."

"Wearing these," I say as I hold my purple crystal.

"Of course."

I raise my eyebrows. "Unfair advantage?"

He leans his face to my head and kisses the top of my black hair. "Devils walk among us, Aestrangel. In all shapes and forms. And don't be fooled by the glamour. There are many limitations we face in this form. For one thing, try not to die, 'cause, well, you really will," he pauses, thinking about his next clever sentence, but he stares at me in the mirror. Longingly? Lovingly? Jealously? "You look so much like her," he sighs.

"Like who?" I question.

"Lilith. My mother."

I run my fingers through my jet-black mane, tucking the stray strands behind my ear. I do resemble her, and it hits me Malek resembles her too. He chooses his shape because it mirrors his mother's human form, but I know the truth, and I have a sense of what lurks underneath. I know he probably takes after his father more than anything.

I wiggle out from under his arm. "And memories? Are you sure we don't..."

He sighs, aggravated he must explain himself to me again. "There are no family ties, no manipulated memories. Whatever we choose to say to the humans becomes our story. The fabricated tale of our history. Callings are to be brief and as inconspicuous as possible. This is your Calling, so everything is up to you. Lucifer thought it best if I tagged along because..."

"I'm not quite angel, not quite demon," I repeat matter-of-factly.

"Exactly. See, we make a good pair!"

I roll my eyes in a very human-like way. "So, what is it? What is this Calling I'm about to go on?"

"Well," he starts, "on this Wild West Tour we'll be camping along-side a bunch of other young people. They're all there to get the ultimate nature experience like us, but all are there for vastly distinct reasons. The human emotion scale finds comfort in distractions, and this trip is the perfect destination for anyone going through a human catastrophe. There will be one couple who is going on this adventure to not only find themselves as individuals, but as a couple. See, Jessica Blackburn and Scott Westmark have been together forever. They were high school sweethearts who evolved into college lovers and are now at the preci-pice of where to go from here. They're twenty-five and at a serious life-changing impasse. Scott hasn't been the most faithful of mates, and while Jess has never confronted him about it, she knows of his constant infidelities."

"Yet, she still wants to be with him?"

"This is their last ditch effort to repair their broken relationship."

My eyes widen. This is easy! I don't see the harm in... "Oh, so I'll need to help them fix things? Get them back on track?"

Malek sucks in air through his teeth with a grating sound that irri-tates my ears. "Uhm..." he trails. "I guess you can say that."

I put a hand on my hip and shift my weight to one leg. How could I ever be so stupid as to think anything involving Lucifer the Father of Lies would be that simple?

"What's the catch, Malek?" I say, my hip bouncing uncontrollably.

"Well," he begins, his voice hoarse and shaky, "Jess and Scott are at a critical moment in their lives together. They're basically at the point of no return."

"And..." I probe, tapping my foot on the wood floor.

"Let's say Jess is unhappy. Very unhappy. And the only solution she can come up with is to... well... she plans on killing Scott during this trip."

My mouth opens on its own, and I freeze in my tracks. "Ok. Not a problem. I can work with that. I must stop her, right? Convince her not to go through with it. Maybe guide her down some other less omi-nous road?"

Malek pauses. His silence makes my heart stop, and there's a pres-sure at my temples that's causing my vision to blur.

"No," he says. "Your job is to convince her to kill him."

Chapter Nine

WILD WEST TOUR

The sun slowly rises over the rocky horizon, casting a golden glow throughout the mesa. The shadows remind me of my violent dream—the one with the strange angel and all the blood. I haven't dreamed since then, and I'm sincerely hoping not to have another one anytime soon.

I press my forehead against the cold window of the tour van and stare out onto the world that is wakening before my eyes. It's spring, and the majesty of the wakening world is in full bloom. I sigh, both amazed I am here and a part of this wondrous cycle of life, and relieved I am no longer in the fog-gloom world of Asphodel. Malek, along with all of our camping gear, is in the seat an aisle across from me. When I last looked over at him, his head was resting back on the high seat and his eyes were closed. But he wasn't sleeping. I know it was part of his deception plan—the one where he talks and acts and *reacts* like a real person. I can imagine it must be hard for him, being a pure demon and all. He must have had to practice a lot in his human shape—get every facial gesture, every nuance, and every voice inflection just right. For me, I'm not really struggling with the guise at all. In fact, I feel comfortable in human skin. It's as if I have a natural inclination for the form.

The van jostles a little, and my head bounces slightly off the glass. My medallion sways out in front of me and nestles itself back on my chest. I reach for it, caress it. I haven't taken it off since Malek gave it to me. I guess I find it comforting to be cloaked in humanity. It's a little better than being stuck between two worlds. Even though I can feel the extent of my mortality when I wear it, the medallion makes me feel like I belong, like I have a purpose. Besides, I'm not so sure I want to see my true visage right now. Horns and all.

I'm still leery about what my mission will entail, but I must believe there will be a greater good at the end of all things. Like the examples Malek showed me—how we influenced those people—on the surface, the deeds seemed morally wrong, or morally ambiguous, at best. However, in the end, everything worked itself out in a seemingly good capacity. So why wouldn't that be the same here? Once complete, I will be free from the confines of Asphodel, and that's nothing but a positive thing. If there's one thing Lucifer is well-known for, it's his word. He may play with words, or be tricky with the stipulations of his deals, but all in all, he makes good on his promises. Malek's words have stayed with me—he said "leave" Asphodel, that was all. He never said anything about "returning" to Ilarium. Yes, I was quick to pick up on the subtlety of the wordplay. So, if leaving Asphodel is step one, then step two is making my way back to Ilarium, and that's going to be the tricky part.

But a thought runs like ice in my brain. *What if they don't want me? What if I truly am not welcome back?*

I can't let that distract me right now. I must take this one day at a time, one step at a time, one *bump* at a time. The van dips low and lurches forward with the inconsistencies in the dirt road. I look over to Malek, who is, oddly enough, staring right at me. "Almost there," he says over the roar of the bus engine. He's confident, an old pro. I nod my head nervously.

Malek gets us to the meeting point safe and sound. Some more fiendish magic and some more hocus pocus. Before I know it, I am now standing outside some bus station with a backpack fastened around my waist and a ticket in my hand looking at a beige van with the words WILD WEST TOURS painted in orange on the side. I bend over and touch my toes to fully absorb where I am. See, the miracle of it all is that I am standing on the earth—actual land! Taking in my first breath of human air is one of the most glorious experiences of my existence!

It is like I had envisioned it to be. All of my preparation and training brought me to this one moment, and I am thankful. I swear, I almost drop to my knees and praise the Lord for all his magnificence, but the human me—Aestra Forcas—pin-prick the back of my brain and tells me that probably isn't the best idea... decorum-wise, of course.

The Wild West Tour is a small company run by a middle-aged couple, Tara and Steve. They basically take six to eight people at a time for two weeks to explore one of the Earth's most glorious landmarks— The Grand Canyon. One of the selling points of their tour is "Unlike other tours available, The Wild West gives you an up-close and personal experience of the splendor of the natural world while connecting you with people you will be friends with for a lifetime." Apparently, Tara and Steve organize groups by means of age, gender, and even personality in order to have a better sense of community when they're in close quarters with others for an extended period of time. When we arrive at the bus station, there is one other couple who is waiting there—Dylan and Janice—a newlywed couple braving the outdoors for their honeymoon. Tara and Steve tell us there were two other couples joining us on the tour—one will be meeting us at the campsite, and the other is a day behind and will catch up to us as soon as they arrive.

"Not to worry, not to worry," Tara says. She is a short woman with short gray hair and a high-pitched voice. "This won't affect our tour at all. We'll make some adjustments to our last-day agenda but trust me— you won't be missing out on anything!" The smile on her face was comforting to the other couple. The newlywed, Janice, had looked frazzled when Tara said one of the couples would be late, but all was resolved when Tara gracefully took control of the situation. The setback doesn't cause Malek or me any concern because, let's face it, we're not out here for the sightseeing.

The bus pulls into Mather Campground as the sun grows larger in the sky. Steve gets on the bus's public address system and heartily announced, "This is Mather Campground. It was named for the first director of the National Park Service. Mather is the largest campground site in Grand Canyon National Park. We are going to set up camp in the section known as Juniper Loop."

Janice and Dylan are in the seat in front of me, and I can hear her squealing with delight at everything Steve says. This must be her dream honeymoon, her dream vacation with her dream of a husband. On the one hand, I find that to be so sweet—a happy couple starting their new

life together, and yet, there's a side of me that wants to throw up in my mouth. Malek is giggling at me. I must have had a disgusted look on my face, and he finds that amusing. I hate to admit it, but it is a little comical, and I giggle too. Steve goes on to talk about the history of the Mather Site and where the general store is. There's a laundromat, too, but in the interest of being "naturalists" we'll forego all that. He discusses the rules and regulations of the park before letting us go to set up camp.

Malek stands in the aisle and tosses me a canteen. "You ready for this?" he asks.

I shrug my shoulders. "Guess I'm gonna have to be."

We all get off the bus and walk to the open clearing that has been reserved for us. It's basically a circle of dirt surrounded by bushes and trees. To the right of the circle is a wooden picnic table, and to the right of the table is a small metal grill on a rusted metal pole. It obviously has seen many uses in its day. Janice trots ahead of me laughing. Her hands are free of any gear, bag, or package, and like a child she points at all the plants and trees and wildlife in our little area. "Look at that!" she yelps. "Oh, that's sooo bee-you-ti-full!"

"Oh, yeah, that sure is something else!" Dylan cheerily responds as he drags all their belongings across the dirt ground. I can tell in his voice that he's not as enthusiastic about this trip as Janice is, but I gather he's being the dutiful husband and taking joy in seeing his new bride so happy.

Malek walks over to a spot closest to the wooded area and drops the gear. I follow him and start unpacking our supplies. "I'll put up the tent," he says, unzipping a bag.

"*The* tent? Not our *tents*?"

"No, Aestrangel," he replies, "one tent for us to share. Is that a problem?"

I huff at the thought of having to be in such close quarters with him. "I guess there's nothing we can do about it now," I say, the aggravation dripping off every word. "Don't you think that's a little creepy?"

"Hey, you're my sister. We shared a womb together! We can surely share a tent. We have separate sleeping bags if that makes you feel better."

I turn my back to him and cross my arms over my chest. "Yeah," I sigh. "So much better."

A car pulls up next to the parked van, and another couple gets out. Steve scurries over with his clipboard and happily greets them. He looks at his paper, makes some notations, and shakes hands with the couple. There's a tingle in my stomach, like some sort of sensor going off, and my crystal necklace pulls tighter down my neck like a magnet trying to drag me to the ground. My hands get slick with sweat, and I rub them down the sides of my jeans. "The others just got here," I say to Malek out of the side of my mouth.

"Oh yeah? I wonder if they're 'ours'?" he answers, still working on the tent.

I know they're ours. No. Mine. My couple. All mine. All mine to exert the power of words and manipulate them into doing the unthinkable...

I shake my head back and forth as if to shake the thought from my brain.

"Why don't you see? Introduce yourself or something," he suggests.

"No. It's them. I know it," I say matter-of-factly.

"You feel it, don't you?" he says smiling.

I nod and turn to help him finish.

—✠-✠⁜✠-✠—

"We've been doing this for a while now," our guide Tara says as she looks at her husband Steve lovingly. "We both got so tired of the everyday rat race that we decided we wanted to do something we both loved. Not having any children made our lifestyle choice much easier, too. But we've met so many different people from so many different walks of life; it's truly been a blessed and fulfilling experience."

Night has fallen, and we're all sitting around a campfire—Malek and me, Tara and Steve, Newlyweds Janice and Dylan, and Jess and Scott. All in a circle around the fire, yet each "couple" staying close together, still guarded in their own human defenses and uncomfortable-ness.

After I had helped Malek assemble the tent, I opened my sleeping bag and rested. The hard-packed earth felt good against my back, and I must have been in a very deep and dreamless sleep because when I awoke, it was already dark out. I woke up to the smell of firewood burning and food cooking, and I asked Malek why he let me sleep for so long. He told me I had looked so peaceful he didn't want to disturb me. He really is so strange sometimes.

So now we're all together, campers strong, and Tara and Steve have regaled us with tales of their Wild West Tours adventures. An uncomfortable silence filters through the campgrounds, and all I hear is my

breath coming in short, panicked pants, and the cacophony of insects singing their nightly chorus.

"Well," Malek declares, breaking the tension, "I'm Malek Forcas, and this is my twin sister Aestra."

Everyone turns to look at us, and I give a meek smile and quick hand wave.

"We're here for the sheer adventure of it all. I guess you can say we're the thrill-seeking type!"

Everyone laughs an obligatory laugh. But Malek is so dashing and so charming that a part of me thinks their laughter is truly genuine. He knows how to work a crowd, knows the right things to say, knows exactly how to time his responses perfectly. He's done this plenty of times, and he is a master at his craft. I fear if I say anything, it won't be human enough, and they'll see right through my act. I look around the crowd, taking in every one of their faces, watching their expressions, homing in on their human nuances so I can mimic them later. I need to teach myself, groom myself, and come into my own as Aestra Forcas for this short window of time.

"So, where are you guys from?" Janice asks, and I detect a hint of a southern accent in her voice.

"Oh, here, there, and everywhere," Malek answers coolly. "We're military brats, so we bounced around a lot." He lies so easily, so effortlessly. The words come out of his mouth as if they were actual truth. I realize I should probably pay attention to him, not only for the way he crafts his words but also for what he's saying. I get a sense this little "introduce yourself" session is more of a teaching class for me.

From the corner of my eye, I see Scott staring at me. Like, he doesn't take his eyes off me, and I try so hard not to meet his gaze. My medallion feels like a heavy weight against my chest. I grab onto it and tug it away from my shirt to try to relieve some of the pressure.

"Aestra?" Scott says in a faint voice. My head instinctively swivels in his direction. "What a strange name." He makes me uncomfortable, so I look away, back to the fire in the center, but before I do, I catch a glimpse of Jess's face, and she doesn't look so happy with her boyfriend's remark.

Jess laughs out loud and swats at Scott's arm. Her whole body lurches forward, and her long, brown hair sweeps along the dirt floor. Malek smiles a Cheshire cat grin. "So is my name!" he says. And again, everyone laughs their pre-programmed, obligatory human laugh.

"It means 'star'," I say, still focused on the fire.

"Yes, and I'm the king!" Malek chimes in, keeping the mood fresh and light.

Jess goes into even more phony hysterics, but phoniness aside, she is lovely to look at. She has long, chestnut hair and is a package of small features. The word I could use to describe her is "cute." "Now, while we're on the topic of names and formal introductions, I'm Jess Blackburn, and this is my boyfriend Scott Westmark." She smiles as she gestures back and forth from her to him. "Scott and I have been together since 9th grade, so that's how long, honey?" she asks him.

"Eleven years," he answers.

"Oh, geez, that's it?" she says jokingly. "Seems like a lifetime!"

"Yeah, tell me about it," he replies. More obligatory ha-ha's and hee-hee's, but I pick up on a slight sliver of truth in Scott's side of the banter.

"Ya'll engaged?" Janice asks before taking a bite out of her hot dog.

Jess forces a smile and shakes her head. "Not yet," she pouts, "but we're out here to have an enjoyable time and see a little bit of the world we wouldn't normally see. We live in New York, so being in the city all the time can be stressful and hectic, and we needed some time to decompress and reconnect. Right, babe?" She motions for Scott to respond, but his attention is fixated on something else... someone else.

Me.

"Babe?" Jess probes, tapping on his leg.

"What? Oh, yeah, yeah," he stammers, breaking his stare from me. "Wall Street is very stressful," he agrees half-heartedly.

Jess frowns in disapproval of his inattentiveness and shoots me a wicked look.

Wait! Did I just become the enemy?

"Excuse me," I say as I stand.

Malek looks at me with concern. "You okay?" he asks.

He starts to get up to follow me, but I put out my hand to stop him. "Just need more water, I'll be right back." As I start to walk to the cooler by the van, I hear Janice say, "Well, I guess it's our turn now!" in her bubbly, irritating voice. I try tune her out until I'm out of range and can't hear her babble anymore.

The back door to the van is open. I sit next to the cooler, lean my body against the back row of seats, and fish in a sea of ice for an unopened bottle of water. I need to breathe. Need to take this all in. I must be student and actress and teacher and sister and friend and

enemy and angel and human and demon all at once, and it's all I can do from keeping my head from exploding.

"Relax," I tell myself, trying to will myself out of a near panic attack. "Everything is going to be fine."

But is everything going to be fine?

The only thing I can be sure of is my need to find out the truth. I know something happened between my time at The Observatory and when I woke up in actual time. I need to fill in the blanks. There's no doubt about that. But to what end? What will the ultimate outcome of this mission be?

I open the cap on the bottle and take a sip of the water. The cool liquid fills my mouth and slides down my throat, and my tense muscles start to relax until a voice breaks through my temporary serenity.

"Wanna pass me one of those," the voice says, startling me.

I look up, and through the darkness, I see Scott walking toward me, never taking his eyes off mine.

CHAPTER TEN

SCOTT

For a second I freeze, unflinching in the soft dome light of the open van. Not only did Scott's voice break the calmness in my mind, but it also jarred me in a deeper way, as if the bass of its deep tones shook me to my core. I realize I don't like his voice. There's something unsettling in the sound—something my human ears can't handle. Or maybe it's my non-human ears picking up on some otherworldly aspect of his being? But then again, Malek is an "unreal" person, and I'm never affected negatively by *his* voice. In fact, Malek's voice is rather soothing, and dreamy. Either way, bottom line is this—since this Scott character first laid eyes on me, he's given me the creeps. Period. The end.

He points at the cooler beside me and smiles. "I'll take one, cold water please, ma'am," he says with a charming voice.

I blink my eyes rapidly, trying to think of an appropriate, human response.

"A water?" he repeats and motions again to the open cooler.

"Oh, yeah, yeah, sure!" I say, shaking my head.

He laughs, not only with his deep voice but also with his strange, crystal-blue eyes. "You okay, there, girl?" He smiles again, but his face is twisted with an odd look.

I grab a bottle and hold it out toward him. "Oh, I'm fine," I say. "Just tired from the long day and all. Guess I was kinda spacing out."

"I'd say!" He laughs again, and this time I respond in kind. "Looked like you were in some other world or something."

I shrug my shoulders. "Something," I say. I stand, still holding the water and take a step forward to meet him halfway. My hope is he'll take the water, I'll take a step back and sit back in the van, and he'll turn on his heels, say thank-you, and go back to camp.

But it doesn't happen that way.

Scott takes a step forward and reaches for the bottle in my hand. As he takes it from me, his thumb brushes on top of my thumb—gently and purposefully. He glides his thumb over the top of mine, smoothing over my thumbnail as if to inspect it. Before I get a chance to pull away from his eerie gesture, flashes of light fire off around me. I know it's happening inside my mind, and only I can see it, but it rocks me and makes me stagger back to the van. He's speaking to me, but I can't hear him. I can only make out specks of his face and the subtle movement of his lips because interspersed between the onslaught of the flashing lights and the reality of Scott before me, I see something *else*... One. Two. Three. Four. I count the flashes as they flicker, yet every time another light bursts, another scene flashes behind it—something horrifying and disturbing.

Flash, then blood-covered dandelions.

Flash, then a torn body ripped from the belly up.

Flash, then miles of human limbs strewn across a green field.

Flash, then a violent storm barreled through a rural city.

Flash, then a red moon hung low in the night.

Flash, then clouds rained blood as humans wept face-up to the sky.

Flash, then a black smoke hand from the Underworld slithers around my throat and applies a diabolical pressure that leaves me choking...

I begin a coughing fit, and as soon as they began, the assault of images ceases, and I'm left holding my head in my hand, rubbing at my temples. Scott holds my arm at my elbow and guides me to sit next to the cooler in the back of the van.

He sits next to me. "Whoa!" he says, wide-eyed. "You okay there?" There is genuine concern in his voice, and I nod my head. But his voice is hollow—off. There's a timbre to it that speaks to my *de-gelic* essence, making me uneasy and twitchy.

"Yeah," I lie, and the lie comes so easily because, *no*, I'm *not* okay. "I don't know what... I guess I got light-headed."

"Drink some more water," he says, handing me his bottle. "You're probably dehydrated. Have you eaten anything?"

I try to think of the appropriate response, but I'm still reeling from the images. There was a strong, malevolent presence in those visions, and underneath my glamoured guise, I can feel my wingtips shaking with distress, which in turn makes my human form jitter in fear.

"I'll take that as a 'no,'" he says.

"I'm fine. I'm fine," I say. "I need to relax for a minute."

He puts a hand on my knee. "Hey, I'll stay here 'til you feel better, okay?" He smiles at me again, and his big blue eyes shine bright like two rare gems in his face. He's not my mission, not my Calling, but he's a part of it. And while my initial instinct is to tell him I'm okay and he doesn't need to stay, I must somehow incorporate him into the plan.

I place my hand on top of his and lightly squeeze his fingers together. "Thank you," I say. "I don't know what I would have done if..."

"I know! You could have fallen and cracked that little head right open!"

We both chuckle a little. Human obligations. But the laughter doesn't last long, and we return to being two strangers in the wilderness.

"So," he begins after a few seconds of uncomfortable silence, "what brings you and your brother out here? I mean, you want adventure and stuff, but there's got to be more to it."

"Uh, not really," I say. "Malek and I have a very strange relationship, to say the least."

Scott pulls his shoulders back a little. "What do you mean, *strange*?"

"Well, we didn't have the traditional upbringing, so to speak. Ya know, growing up military has its drawbacks. So, it seems he and I are always kinda chasing something down. Almost like we need to be in constant motion. Go. Go. Go."

He squeezes my knee and a flash of light fires off again. I look at Scott's face, and his eyes are gouged out. Blood flows from his eye sockets and down his cheeks. I jump, startled. He removes his hand, and his face goes back to normal.

"Okay, okay," he says calmly, "dehydrated and paranoid!"

I huff and shake my head. "Oh stop!" I say, blowing my mini freak-out off.

"For someone who claims to like adventure and danger, you sure are jumpy."

"Now, wait a second," I defend. "Adventure and danger are two very different things!"

"You think it's possible to have one without the other?" he asks.

I think about that for a moment. "I'm sure it's possible in some capacity. Yes, I do enjoy adventure, but that doesn't mean I want to kill myself in the process." I think about what Malek said about dying—how I can't do it because I would truly *die*. Makes me question why he would send me on an assignment in a very risky area of the world.

"Can't argue with you there," he says. "But sometimes it's about recognizing the danger when there isn't an adventure attached to it."

His words make me pause, and my insides pull back a bit. I had been too busy chitter-chattering, impressing myself with the ease at which I was able to piggy-back off Malek's story, and pre-occupied with those body-rocking visions, that my preternatural instincts had all but canceled out the creepiness in Scott's voice I had initially felt.

Uneasily, I try to shift the focus from me to him, ignoring his ominous words. "What brings you and your girlfriend out here, then?" I ask, desperately trying to conceal my alarm.

He repositions himself and shifts around nervously. "Well, ya know. It's kind of the same reason why you're here. We're looking for something to fill some empty spaces in our lives."

Or do you mean, in your relationship?

"When you work crazy hours six days a week, a lot can get lost in the shuffle." He extends his arms over his head and breathes in the Canyon air. "But being out here, in the middle of all this," he relaxes his arms back to his sides, "it's enough to get a person all recharged and ready for round two."

"Ready for round two?"

"In the boxing match of life."

I smirk at his response because it so easily matched mine.

Too easily.

A rustling in the trees beyond the van makes me jolt. Scott grabs my knee again and "shushes" me like a weak and scared child. Hot anger starts to rise in me but cools down when I see it's Malek emerging from the woods.

"Hey sis!" he says coolly. "Been wondering where you went off to."

I over-exaggerate a smile for him. "Been right here the whole time," I answer matter-of-factly.

"With some company, I see."

Malek locks eyes with Scott in an awkward, territorial-like glare. I can feel the intensity of Malek's authority over him, and in no time, Scott backs down by blinking and looking at his hand on my knee. I assume Malek's eye-storm got the best of Scott, and he succumbed to Malek's unearthly power.

"If you're okay, I'm gonna get on back over to Jess," Scott says, practically stammering. He pats my knee one last time and stands.

"Yeah, I'm all good," I say as he starts walking past Malek.

"Yeah, man, she's fine!" Malek yells to Scott's back.

"Thank you!" I call out to him, hoping to lessen the blow of Malek's mental win over him.

Scott raises his hand up in the air to acknowledge me but doesn't answer or look back.

Malek smirks and joins me in the back of the van.

"What the hell was that about?" I growl at him when Scott is safely out of earshot.

Malek giggles like a little schoolkid. "Aw, c'mon, just having a little fun!"

I turn my head from him. "No, it's not just a little fun, Malek! You didn't have to do that."

"Do what?" he asks sarcastically, as if he doesn't realize the malice of his actions.

"You totally freaked him out!" I say.

He waves his hands in the air. "He completely deserved it."

"Yeah, but now he probably thinks there's something more to us, like you're jealous or something. And maybe he won't believe our story, and I won't get to finish my mission, and..." I'm out of breath, frantic.

"Relax," he says, combing back my hair. "If anything, I'm the over-protective brother. The story is intact, I assure you. Which, by the way, I commend you greatly! You're kinda a natural at this!"

"You heard?"

"Every word, my dear. Handled it all like a pro."

I blush, ashamed I could fabricate a story so easily, so naturally. So, if Malek was close enough to be listening to my conversation, then maybe he was close enough to see me stumble and go into a trance! I sit up stiff and straight. "Did you see it? Did you see me have a freak-out attack?"

He nods.

"So... what was all that about? What the hell was with the lights and images and all that... that... disgusting stuff. I've seen those things

before—like they were memories, or dreams, or things to come. I don't know."

Malek folds his hands together and raises them to his chin. "It's all of that, and so much more. Were you scared by any of it?"

I shake my head. "At first. Only because I had no warning, and they overtook me quickly. But no, they stressed me out more than anything. I'll tell you what, I was more disturbed by Scott than the visions," I huff.

"How so?" he asks, but I know he knows the answer. I know Malek wants me to reveal things for myself because it will make me stronger in my Calling.

Give a man a fish, and he can eat for a day. Teach a man to fish, and he can eat for a lifetime.

"I can't explain it."

"Try," he coaxes.

I close my eyes, recalling the image of Scott's face—his light blue eyes, his short blond hair. I remember the feeling in my spine every time he spoke, like a thousand needles tapping into the core of my otherworldly body. Being around him felt like pinpricks. Like fragments of glass grinding into the soles of my feet. "It was like Asphodel," I say, my eyes still closed. "Like something empty. Missing. There's a feeling of constant longing. Mourning? No, not mourning, that's not the right word. It's a wanting. A deep-seated yearning."

I open my eyes, and Malek is beaming like a human child on Christmas morning. "What?" I say, confused. "What did I say?"

"Who's your Calling?" he asks me, still smiling.

"The girl. Jessica Blackburn," I answer like a soldier repeating orders.

"What is your Calling?"

I cock my head to the side as if to say, *You're not really going to make me say it, are you?*

Malek understands my gesture and nods. "I'm surprised it doesn't make sense to you, Aestrangel. Even though you are doused in a humanity-suit, doesn't mean you have to completely submerge yourself in it. You're going to have to use your powers every now and then."

I stare at the ground in front of us. "De-gelic," I say, and in my mind's eye, I can see him smiling away, so proud of his little devil prodigy.

"Ahhh, I like what you did there..." he coos.

"Not quite demon..."

"Not quite angel."

Malek pats me on the back. "Scott is Marked. He's been Marked since the moment of his birth. It was written in his *Astral Gene*—that little transcendent spark that resides in all humankind—that he would cross paths with you at some point in his life, Aestrangel. When he touched you, and you saw the visions, you were seeing through time and beyond. Those scenes happened, but they haven't happened yet. They were your memories and visions of future events intertwined at once. When he touched you, his humanity wouldn't allow him to be graced with the visions, but he's drawn to you because he was meant to cross paths with you. What fragments are left of his soul *yearns* for you—*has been yearning* for you from the second he existed as a person on this planet. That's how you know he's the right one. That's how you know you're on the right path."

"But I don't understand! He's not my Calling."

"Yes, but the actions you influence upon your Calling, the right path you are to set her upon, will in turn determine his fate."

I turn my head and look at him. "I'm so confused right now; I don't know if I would know the right path if it was laid out in gold before me."

He cups his hand under my chin and tilts my head so my eyes directly catch his gaze. The beautiful cave on the beach is within them. I hate to admit it, but Malek really does an excellent job of calming me down, and unlike anyone else, he seems to be the only one who gets me. With his free hand, he slowly traces a line down the center of my chest, caressing the flesh and outline of bone on my upper-chest, grazing along the inner curves of my womanly shape. I get a shiver—a human shiver makes my human skin-shell blossom with gooseflesh. He reaches my medallion and grabs onto it, sending a warm wave of peace throughout my chest. "The path is there, Aestrangel," he silently says. "You just can't see it yet. But you will. Very, very soon."

His eyes take me away, back to the beach where Samael and Lilith are wrapped in a tight embrace along the shore.

CHAPTER ELEVEN

DAY TRIP

You can learn a lot about someone by watching them sleep. For some reason, I can't stop watching Malek as he sleeps in the sleeping bag beside me. My eyes go in and out of focus as I watch his chest rise and fall with every breath he takes. Each one of his exhales comes with a puff of chilly morning air, but my otherworldly senses know that's part of the glamour. To the human eye, it's a natural reaction to the low air temperatures, but I know the truth. It is the smoky breath of a foul demon recharging his powers in his slumber. I envision him as his true self. I pick up the fragments and pieces of what I did see, and my humanness conjures the rest—designing a hideous beast from the darkest of nightmares.

But he can't be! Because I look at his handsome countenance wrapped peacefully in the throes of slumber, and I think about his charming presence and his soothing voice and his stormy eyes, and I think—for a split second—I think I kinda swoon over him. I shake my hands out, hoping to shake away the feeling, unzip the tent, and step out into the cold morning air.

The women of the group are awake and busily preparing breakfast. Tara is kneeling by the frying pan, and Janice and Jess are organizing paper plates and utensils for the camp. The smell of eggs, bacon, and coffee intermingle with the woodland scent of the crisp Canyon air. I extend my arms above my head, elongating my body in a satisfying, bone-popping stretch. "Can I help with anything?" I offer through a yawn.

Janice and Jess turn toward me. Janice smiles brightly, Jess quickly looks away. "Mornin'!" Janice beams. "You feelin' any better?"

I rub my eyes, and my brain scrambles to figure out what she means. *Last night. Scott must have told them I almost fainted.*

"Oh, yeah," I reply. "Just needed to sleep it off."

"That's good," Tara chimes. "Wouldn't want to have to bench you from the day's activities."

I bend forward at my waist and stretch out my back. My medallion dangles out in front of me, dangerously close to the ground. "Nope, wouldn't want that," I mumble.

"Aestra, come help me with this, please," Tara says as she stands. I walk over to her spot and kneel before the frying pan staring into a mound of yellow scrambled eggs covered in a dark orange cheese sauce. She hands me a spatula. "Don't let them get too overcooked."

Even though I have no idea what she means, I nod my head, take the spatula and start prodding at the food.

Tara takes her cellphone out of her back pocket, looks at it and frowns. "Oh well. Looks like we're gonna have to hold off one more day."

Janice whips her head around. "What do you mean?" she whines.

"The other couple texted me," Tara continues. "They're not gonna make it here until tonight."

Janice puts the coffee pot on the picnic table and huffs. "Seriously? That's like two days wasted now!" She puts her hands on her hips and shakes her right leg like an impatient child.

"Oh relax!" Jess scolds as she walks by her.

Tara puts her phone back in her pocket. "Jess is right. They're a young couple, and they're going through an unimaginable time right now, so I'm okay with giving them a little slack."

My ears perk up. "Why? What's up with them?"

"Well, last winter, they lost their seven-month-old daughter to SIDS—Sudden Infant Death Syndrome. It's been really rough for them, and this tour was supposed to bring them some healing. They need to get away on many distinct levels. Especially the mom—she's in a very deep depression."

Janice relaxes her stance. Her facial expression changes from annoyed to concerned in the blink of an eye. "Oh," she sighs, putting her hand over her chest. "That's so sad. I can't even imagine how that must feel. I mean, Dylan and I just got married and all, but we've been together for a while, and we've discussed all that stuff. I'm really looking forward to having lots of babies with him! And the thought of going through all that planning and excitement just to..." Her voice trails, and she shakes her head. "I don't even want to think about it!"

"Steve and I never had any children, so I wouldn't know what that's like, either. But I agree, it must be absolutely devastating," Tara adds before returning to her tent.

Suddenly, I feel a presence behind me. "Let me do that," Jess snarls. I turn to look at her, and she's scowling at me. Her blue eyes are darkened with disgust. "You're doing it wrong. They're gonna stay watery if you keep doing that."

I look at the frying pan with the eggs in it and back at Jess before standing up. "Have at it," I say, pointing the spatula at her, thankful I have been relieved of my duties.

She glares at me hard and snatches the spatula out of my hand. A lump forms in my throat—one of reservation and fear.

"So, Jess," Janice pries. "What about you and Scott? What are your plans? Are there little kiddos in your future?"

Jess pauses reflectively as all female eyes are now on her. I go out on a limb and assume this is the type of conversation women my age engage in often. Plans for the future. Companionship. Marriage. Children. Repopulating the world with a new crop of worshippers for the Lord. *Or a new crop of devils for The Morning Star, depending on which way you look at it.* By the look on Jess's face, this is a topic of distress—one she's probably discussed at length with her family, her best friends, and Scott, *ad nauseam.* And I predict the outcome is always the same... her not-so-doting boyfriend gives her excuse after excuse as to why they can't—as the people say—tie the knot.

"I'd be happy with a ring at this point," she finally answers, leaving an uncomfortable feeling hanging heavy in the air.

Janice lets out a nervous little chuckle. "Well, who knows?" she smiles, her words dripping with feigned positivity. "Maybe this trip will be the push in the right direction for you guys?"

"Yeah," Jess mumbles, staring deep into the frying pan. "We'll see."

Janice turns her attention toward me like a laser-beam. "What about you, Aestra? Seeing anyone? Thinking about marriage or kids?"

The questions take me off guard, as I am, obviously, not equipped to answer them. As if on cue, Malek unzips our tent and steps outside, stretching and yawning in the very same fashion as I did. Seeing him sparks my imagination and the lie filters out. "Oh no! When you have to deal with someone like him," I motion my head in Malek's direction, "on a daily basis, it's kinda enough to ruin your desire to procreate."

Janice, Jess, and Tara start to giggle as Malek smiles wide. "What?" he asks as if he's missed something important, to which we all giggle even more. Typical human female behavior. He winks at me, and I know he knows he just saved my butt. "Oh, I get it," he says. "Girl talk. No guys allowed. Is that what's going on here?"

"Something like that," Jess says, perking up at Malek's arrival. The tone of her voice changed. *Shifted.* Like there was a touch of curiosity in it when Malek spoke. As a matter of fact, her face brightened when she saw him smiling, as if she had forgotten about her tense relationship with Scott for a split second and was completely enthralled by... *Oh, no way, Jessica, you're mine. You're my mission, and you better not get any ideas about.*

"You didn't let my sister cook any of that, did you?" he says over Jess's shoulder.

Jess giggles again, a little louder this time, a little more *flirtatiously* this time. "Oh no," she says, playing along with him. "Tara put her in charge, but I took over right away." She's smiling at him. Big and bright white teeth shining in the morning sun. Her eyes have brightened up too, and with my de-gelic eyes, I see her aura flicker as her guard comes down for him. He winks at her, and she sheepishly dips her chin down to the top of her shoulder.

I walk to Malek, put my hand to his elbow, and guide him to the picnic table. "Har har har," I say dryly, trying to break the moment. "Everything's almost ready. Come, sit."

I sit across from him and stare at him hard as if to ask, "What the hell was that?" but he doesn't flinch at my questioning eyes, he doesn't react to my accusatory gaze. He smiles away and puts his hands on top of mine.

One by one, the others emerge from their tents ready to greet the day, but most importantly, ready to fill their bellies. We all sit together as Tara serves us our food, and Steve passes out maps and itineraries.

"So, Tara told me about the little snafu in the plan," he says. "In all honesty, it's not a big deal at all. We had built in free exploration days to the end of the tour, anyway. I made some quick rearrangements to the schedule, as you'll see, and I think it'll work out for everyone. Don't you worry about nothing! We'll still do everything as planned—the hikes, the river raft, the whole Canyon extravaganza! Today, you're all on your own. We're on the South Rim," he opens his map and points to our location, "so you're probably going to want to stay local. Take your maps with you if you decide you want to explore. This way you won't get lost. If you go to the Visitor Center, it's a five-minute walk straight to the Canyon. You can explore the Rim Trail as time permits. Or there's a shuttle bus that comes around every hour to the Visitor Center to do quick stops at the Canyon's 'hot spots.' Feel free to shower, shave, or shop for souvenirs. Rest and relax if you want. The forecast calls for some light rain in the afternoon, but it shouldn't be too bad. Tomorrow, we head out on the Bright Angel Trail on our way to Phantom Ranch." Again, he points at the map, drawing his finger down a red line from point A to point B.

"So, what are ya'll thinking about doing today?" Janice cheerily addresses the group.

Jess leans her head on Scott's shoulder. "Well," she says speaking to us, but looking dreamily at him, "since we are gonna be in for a busy hike tomorrow, I was thinking we could maybe do what Steve suggested—rest and relax? Maybe read a little in our books, listen to some music, or..."

Scott pulls back a little and says, "Uh, I was thinking of maybe checking out the Rim Trail, if you didn't mind."

Jess lifts her head, stunned. "Oh," she answers tersely.

"I like that whole rest and relaxation idea," Janice interrupts. "Me and Dylan are probably going to do the shuttle tour."

Dylan sips his coffee and nods obediently.

"Well, I'm with you!" Malek bellows as he looks at Jess. "We have a lot of excitement headed our way, and I think you got the right idea!"

A smile sprouts on her face, and I kick Malek's leg under the table. Scott looks at me, and his eyes pierce through mine as I anticipate what he's going to say. Malek kicks me back, urging me to say something. I stammer, like an idiot.

"Wanna head to the Rim Trail, Aestra?" Scott asks. "Going in pairs is better than going alone."

I'm dumbfounded. All eyes are on me in this very awkward, and very public invitation. If looks could kill, I'd be dead about a thousand times over from Jess's glares.

"And ya kinda owe me for saving your butt last night..." he continues.

Another swift kick from Malek under the table. "I guess you're right," I relent.

—✶—✶※✶—✶—

The Canyon is wide, and the Canyon is deep, and I can scarcely imagine how many different lives it has sucked up within its core. Even though the Rim Trail is outlined in a strong, metal fence, it would be so easy to hoist my body over, or even slightly tap another person clear over the side. But I can't think about that, as that is not my business at hand.

The mid-afternoon heat leaves sweat droplets all around my hairline and neck. It's irritating, and I try desperately to sweep my hair into some kind of bun contraption at the top of my head to no avail.

"Here," Scott says, handing me a rubber band from his pocket. "Use this. It might help."

I can't trust his smile. I see right through the simple act of kindness. I pick up on his phony intentions. It's almost as if he isn't real. Like he's a shell of a person, with barely a blip of a soul residing in his body. I reach my hand out anyway, accepting his gift. The rubber band is wrapped around his right forefinger, and the only way for me to take it is to loop my finger around it. I try to be quick about it, attempting not to make physical contact, but it's no use. Not only do my fingers graze his, but I stumble forward.

He catches me with his left arm and steadies me in place against his chest. "Whoa! Whoa! You sure you're feeling up for this?" he jokes.

My head is nestled against his chest, and the sound of his hollow voice resonates in my head. He squeezes my hand, making me woozy. Sick. I realize my medallion is pressed between our chests, and I can feel its power encircling the both of us like a smoky blanket. I close my eyes and listen to his heartbeat. It sounds like a dull, rhythmic drum—strong, but slow beating.

Thum. Thump. Thum. Thump.

I see a vision of the angel with the razor wings. This time she is floating above the Canyon's opening. Her arms are wide open, inviting someone for an embrace, but her hands are no longer hands. They are

metal contraptions with gears and spikes and spinning saw blades. Her black hair covers her face, again, but I can see through the black strands that she is smiling—a diabolical grin.

Welcome death with opened arms, I think, and Scott mumbles something back that is unintelligible. Did he hear me?

The angel glides closer to me, and I see there are objects embedded in the spikes of her mechanical hands. They look like small, white globes with pale blue marbles in the center. But as she gets closer, I realize they are not globes, but rather they are eyes.

Human eyes.

Scott's eyes.

Frightened, I jump back. Scott makes a motion to prevent me from falling, but I am out of his reach. "I, uh... I don't think I feel too well. Maybe this wasn't such a promising idea. I think I need to go back to camp."

I kept my distance the entire walk back to camp. A part of me was afraid of making bodily contact with him again because I didn't want to be bombarded with more images. Scott spoke to me the entire time, his voice like dissonant chimes echoing off the Canyon walls. It was hard to listen to him, hard to pay attention to his questions, when all I heard was the howling of his vocal cords. But I answered as best and as succinctly as I could. I don't think he appreciated my abruptness, but he's not my Calling, and I really wanted to keep my distance. Malek said he was Marked, and while I'm not exactly sure what that means, I don't like the way it sounds—or feels.

When we arrive back at the campsite, the sun is already starting to set. Tara, Steve, Malek and Jess are getting dinner ready for the group. I excuse myself to my tent so I can be alone for a little bit before Janice and Dylan get back and we gather for our nightly pow-wow.

I must have drifted to sleep because the next thing I know, Malek is crouching over me in the tent. "This human thing is really taking its toll on you, isn't it? I think you've slept more than you've been awake."

I rub my eyes. "How long have I been out?"

"Not long." He pats me on the head. "Come on! Dinner is ready, and Steve's getting his guitar."

I roll my eyes. "Great," I mumble.

"You'll have to tell me all about your little excursion later."

"There's absolutely nothing to tell."

His face twists. "No visions? No handholding? No..."

I sit up. "No nothing." And I follow him out of the tent.

The group is in a circle around a fire, like last night. "There she is! Miss Sleepyhead!" Steve proclaims as I sit next to Malek in the circle. The others in the group give little cheers and a welcoming applause.

"I know, I know," I say, brushing him off.

"So, everyone have a good day today?" he asks as he strums a few notes on his guitar.

We all nod, mumble, mutter. Half-hearted responses for an uneventful day. I'm second-guessing this whole Calling business because wouldn't it have made more sense for me to stay back with Jess, rather than to have gone with Scott?

Headlights shine in the distance, and Tara jumps up from the ground. "They're here!" she exclaims, and a car rounds a corner and parks next to The Wild West van. The couple gets out of the car, and Tara races to them, throwing her arms around the neck of the woman. "I'm so glad you guys made it okay. You are okay? Right?" The woman laughs and tosses her shoulder-length brown hair behind her. "Come on," Tara continues. "We're about to have something to eat, and you need to get acquainted with the rest of the gang!"

The three walk over to the circle, and I am immediately drawn to the woman right away. There's a strange movement in her hip that strikes me as odd, like she had a fall of sorts. *I know she's gone through a mental and emotional tragedy, but is she even physically fit to be on a vacation like this?*

Tara ushers the two into the circle but safely away from the fire. "Okay, everyone. These are the two we've been waiting for! Everyone, this is Logan and Reba Callaghan."

They smile and wave, and we all wave back.

Tara starts pointing around the circle, introducing us one by one. "Logan, Reba, this is Janice and her husband Dylan, Jess and her boyfriend Scott, and Aestra and her brother Malek."

Nod, wave, nod, wave, but Reba stops when she gets to me. She gives me a soft, knowing smile. Against the shadows of the dancing firelight, her face glows with a white aura that is soothing, comforting, *familiar.*

"Hello, Aestra," she says in a wispy voice, and I nearly double over in shock.

"Hi, Reba," I say weakly, desperately trying to hide my emotions, because Logan and Reba Callaghan are not really Logan and Reba Callaghan.

Hello, Revalia, I wish to say, but I keep my mouth closed and make room for my old friends.

CHAPTER TWELVE

CONFRONTATIONS

Revalia and her companion glide to a spot in the circle across from me. It seems as if her feet barely touch the ground. To these other humans here in the camp, she's one of *them*—a living, breathing person who was born approximately twenty-five years ago, grew up, and will eventually die as they will. But I can see through her veil. She hasn't been a human for awfully long, and while she seems to have a handle on the feel of the mortal shell, there's still a flicker of divinity that dances around her body, giving her angelic aura away. *Her companion has it too.* I study them long and hard, and it doesn't take me long to figure out that 'Logan' is Lozhure.

I sit up straight at attention, wanting to rush over to her, embrace her with my angel wings, kiss her face, and smother her in my love and gratitude.

She came! She came to help me! She came to save me!

From the corner of my eye, I catch Malek's facial expression, and in an instant, my overwhelming feelings of jubilation come crashing down. His jaw is locked tight. His cheekbones are clenched so hard they jut out like chiseled ridges on the sides of his face. And his eyes... my word, his eyes could raise tidal waves that could sink the Canyon for

eons! His eyes have blackened with fury like I've never seen because he knows—he knows who and what they are, and I'm sure this is a bump in the road he had not anticipated. And that's when I realize: She came! She came to help me! She came to save me!

Because they think I'm weak.

Weak. Like, I can't do this on my own. Like, I'm so stupid, dumb, helpless, hopeless, and incompetent that I need not one, but *two* angels to assume the mortal coil and usher me to salvation! Am I *their* Calling? The one Camael said was unprecedented in the history of the Angelic Order? I feel sick as the conversation Revalia and Lozhure had in my hand-created orb comes back to me: *It can't be Aestra. You know that. She's weak. She could never punch through time and space like that. No. Wherever she is, she's far away from here, and her weakness couldn't even wish to reach us. Not here. Not anywhere.*

My eyes narrow, and I continue to stare them down. Reba and Logan, or shall I say Revalia and Lozhure, introduce themselves and start making small talk with the group, but I tune them out. Their words sound like the wheels of a freight train pounding against a metal track. I take deep breaths to control the rage building in my chest. How dare they? I'm not weak! I'm *here*, aren't I? *Here* on earthly soil, doing anything and everything I can to make it back to Camael, back to Ilarium, back to *the Lord* so I can right whatever wrongs I may—or may not have—committed! Because, until I know the truth for sure, I cannot and will not admit any wrongdoing on my part. I was thrust into this situation with no recollection of my actions, and therefore, I am unable to assess what happened to me. I will not be judged *or* punished until all the facts are made known to me. Weak? Revalia is so misguided she's been brainwashed to confuse ingenuity and perseverance for weakness. Weak? *She's* the weak one, obviously! She's so weak that she needed to be sent down to Earth with a companion angel to help her along. Guess she's not strong enough to get the job done on her own and...

Malek places a calming hand on my knee, silencing my inside tirade. He must sense my growing fury as well. I place my hand on top of his to let him know that *I* know and am completely aware of the situation. I squeeze his fingers to let him know that I too, am disturbed by their arrival. From my peripheral view, I see him nod his head. *He got my message.*

It's interesting to see Revalia as Reba. It's like looking at some warped version of the angel I once knew—the non-concrete form she once inhabited has gelled together into a concrete, touch-able state. The fragments of her non-corporeal essence have organized into a cohesive and real person. Yet, she still shimmers and sparkles with hints of her angelic breath these other people can't detect. But they smile at her and seem to be entranced by her presence. Maybe their own Astral Genes, the little slivers of divinity given to every human, are drawn to Revalia and Lozhure, but they don't know why.

I'm barely paying attention to what's happening within the group when I hear Tara say, "Is that okay with you, Aestra?"

I pep up and regain my focus on the present. "Huh? What?" I say, tuning in.

"Would you mind showing Reba where the supplies are in the van while Scott and Dylan help Logan with his tent?"

Malek slips his hand away from my grasp and motions for me to go. I've learned not to believe in coincidences anymore, so I nod my head in agreement and get up. Revalia smiles at me as I lead the way to the van.

When we're out of earshot, Revalia rushes close to me as if to throw her arms around me for a human embrace. She stops dead in her tracks and backs up when she notices the medallion around my neck. She breathes in, composing herself. "You're here," she says, beaming.

I run my hand through my hair, trying to smooth down any feelings of fury from within. "Yep," I answer tersely. "So are you. And Lozhure, too."

"We're going to help you, Aestra. We're going to help get you out of here and away from that demon!"

I huff with contempt. "Malek? He's harmless. Not an issue."

Her brows furrow. She extends her arm out to me, maybe hoping I will hold her hand, but I ignore the gesture. "Aestra," she says with a concerned tone. "The more you stay in his presence, the more you will be corrupted by his actions and his words."

I shrug my shoulders. Her holier-than-thou attitude irritates me. "I've made it this far. I'm fine."

"But you're not fine, Aestra! Lozhure and I..."

"Lozhure and you *what*? Came here to save me from the clutches of the big bad demon? Came here to save my soul?" My voice rises, echoing among the trees.

She looks over her shoulder like a frightened child to see if anyone heard us, or if anyone is approaching. "Aestra!" she pleads, and something about the sound of her voice is so pathetic I think my heart may

have softened a bit. I realize she's here to do her job. She's here on unquestioned orders from her superiors. And that, to me, is a little sad—sad that she hasn't been able to carve out her own way for her existence, sad that she accepts the fate that was handed to her from the dawn of her being, sad that she has no other thought in her head but to love and serve the Creator with every fiber of her soul.

"Listen, Lia," I say, calmly. "I don't need your rescuing or saving. I'm okay. Really. Truly. I can do this on my own. I need to do this on my own. Do you understand?"

Her eyes indicate to me she doesn't. She has no clue what it feels like. Yes, this poor creature has been through her own personal hell and back, but she's never walked amongst the fog beasts of the Underworld. Literally.

"I know the path I've chosen will lead me to the answers I seek," I continue. "It will lead me to remember what happened to me."

She shakes her head, confused. "Wait? What don't you remember?"

Now I'm a little confused. "How I got here. I mean, I know *how* I got here, but I am unsure about the *why*. Why?"

"You mean, you don't know?" she repeats.

"No. I just said that! The last thing I remember is being in The Observatory with you and Lozhure. And then I was falling for what seemed like an eternity before I ended up in Asphodel. But no. I don't know anything else."

Her eyes open wide in terror. "Aestra, you... you fell from Ilarium because you renounced the Lord. Do you not remember that?"

I clench my fists, readying myself for a battle. "Why? Why did I do that?" I ask coolly, trying to maintain composure. "Why won't you just tell me what happened?"

"I can't. I mean, I'm not able to," she says in a muffled voice. "You made a pact with The Morning Star, and try as I might, that oath is a strong one. The words aren't allowed to leave my mouth, or anyone else's. Lucifer's bond is that strong."

I sigh. My shoulders rise and descend and somewhere inside of me, I can feel my black wings move up and down—the weight of them bearing heavily on me even in my counterfeit human figure. "Then why the hell are you and Lozhure even here? Why did they send both of you on a Calling?" I growl.

"Lozhure is with me because we're a team. He and I," she pauses, choosing her words carefully, "he and I have an agreement with Camael and the other Powers That Be. We aren't dispatched to Callings the way other angels are."

"Because you have both failed before, is that right?" I say sharply. There's a certain malice in my voice that takes even me off guard when it's released from my mouth.

A tear forms at the corner of her right eye. My human words have struck her deeply. "Oh, Aestra," she whimpers. "The Creator is willing to take you back if you repent. You are so special to Him, and He loves you very much. This is not the path He has envisioned for you. Believe it or not, He still loves The Morning Star, too, for you are both His children, His most perfect creations. And nothing—not even the greatest affront to Him could ever change that. If you are truly sorry in your heart, His door is always open to you."

There's a part of me that wants to believe her—that wants to reach out and embrace her and feel comforted in her arms. There's a part of me that wants to scream out "Yes! I repent! I will return with you and forever live in service to Him!" but I can't. Not until I know the truth, and she's made it abundantly clear to me that she is not permitted to give me that information. How can I repent for sins I have no knowledge of committing? When I first came to be in Asphodel, I fell to my knees and screamed for the Lord. I begged forgiveness, yet no one came. So why would that change now?

Her words are thin to me, like a gossamer curtain allowing fragmented morning light to enter a room; thin and hollow—empty promises she cannot commit to keep. I understand I am her Calling—a problem she needs to solve and fix. And I understand her mission: convince me to apologize, and perhaps prevent me from murdering Scott.

"The group is going to hike Bright Angel Trail tomorrow," Revalia says. "That hike will lead us to Phantom Ranch. Phantom Ranch is a lodge run by a woman named Ruth Sterling. She is our Watcher. I want you to meet her, talk to her. Maybe she can give you some other perspective." She looks at my medallion and motions her chin forward. "Its power is enormous. Lozhure, and I could sense it a few miles away. I can see how it would consume you."

"It doesn't consume me!" I bark.

"Oh, it does. And the longer you wear it, the longer you give yourself to it, the more it is likely your soul will forever become trapped within its casing."

I make a *tuh* sound with my mouth, dismissing her comment as nonsense. "We really should get back to the others," I say and turn from her.

She nods and walks at my side. "And even though you walk among the demons, Aestra, the Lord will forgive you. For His love is all powerful and all-encompassing and demands no bargain in return."

More lies?

My heart breaks as we walk back to camp. It breaks for Revalia and Lozhure and all the other angels in Ilarium. It breaks for me, too. If the path to enlightenment is shrouded in lies, why even bother? What has Revalia become? Or rather, what have I become?

When I get back to the tent, Malek is already in his sleeping bag. He's not asleep, though. He's been waiting for me the entire time, waiting to hear my assessment of the "angel invasion." But I have no words for him, yet by the look on his face, he's okay with that. When I sit on my sleeping bag across from him, he reaches for my hands, and I let his icy touch wash over me. We speak no words to each other, yet our knowing eyes speak volumes in tongues I can't decipher, and for the first time, something inside me feels as if it has awoken.

—✕—✕—✳—✕—✕—

A light rain trickles against the tent, but that's not why my eyes have flashed open from sleep. Angry voices shouting in the tent next to ours have jarred me from my dreamless slumber. I look over, and Malek is unfazed. His eyelids flutter rapidly under the spell of his dream. A rush of curiosity consumes me, and I desire to hear more of the unfolding argument, so leave the tent and park myself at the picnic table.

"Why do you always have to be like that?" a man's deep voice yells. *It belongs to Scott.*

"Because," the female whines. *That would be Jess.* "I've been trying to get through to you for so many years now, and I feel like I keep hitting a brick wall!"

"Really? Really? We're gonna play this game now?"

"It's not a game, Scott!"

"Well, it sure feels like one, Jessica! Cut the shit! We're not in high school anymore!"

The zipper to their tent comes down. Jess screams as she exits their tent.

Scott says something back, but it's muffled behind the sound of the zipper going back up.

I turn my head to see Jess standing by the fire pit. She huffs angrily, "Great! We woke you up! You heard all that, didn't you?"

"Eh," I say sheepishly. "Not all of it. I couldn't sleep anyway."

She swats at her eyes, trying to make her tears magically disappear. "Listen," she begins with deep conviction, "I'm just letting you know whatever happened with you and Scott, or whatever was said between the two of you... just... just don't get any ideas, okay?"

"W...what do you mean," I stammer.

"You know what I mean!" she sighs. "Don't get any ideas because no matter what happens, he always comes back to me. In the end, it's all about me." Tears rise in her eyes again.

She looks like a porcelain plate teetering on the edge of a shelf. One push, and she'll come crashing to the tile floor and splinter into a thousand pieces. *I swear, I could kill you! she said.* All I have to do is say the word, and this could be it! Mission accomplished. In and out. And it would be so easy, too. Like Malek said, the power or words, the persuasion of words, is the downfall of man. I have an open opportunity to shake the shelf and move on with my life!

Another opening zipper from another tent distracts me. *Revalia.* I guess her angel instincts haven't gone completely away!

"Everything okay out here?" she calls to us from the opening of her tent.

"Peachy!" Jess calls back to her.

"Okay," Revalia says, and she slinks back inside.

Now's my chance!

I frantically scan my mind for all the possible things I could say that might put Jess over the edge. I think of all the scenarios and images that could hurt her, drive her, motivate her, inspire her to go through with what is in her heart. *He spoke to me inappropriately. He tried to hold my hand. He made a move on me. He tried to kiss me.* Or, I could have very well told her the truth—that her boyfriend is a near-soulless human being who is destined to meet a horrible death, but I don't think she would have appreciated that one either.

One thing I've observed is the human heart is easily swayed—Malek taught me that first-hand! And the way Jess looks right now—standing there with false bravado, thinking she's facing down a potential rival for her mate, protecting what she wants so desperately to believe is hers—I

could present her with any one of those circumstances, and she would come completely unhinged.

"Are you coming back in?" Scott yells from their tent.

Jess cocks her head over her shoulder. "In a minute!" she yells and turns back to me. She puts her hands up on her hips and starts bouncing side to side, waiting impatiently for me to respond.

"It's raining!" he yells back at her, but this time he sounds legitimately concerned for her.

Oh, look at that, I didn't even realize the rain was getting harder.

"I knoooooooow!" she whines again and taps her foot against the dirt.

I open my mouth, but nothing comes out. I hesitate. I can't bring myself to do it, because something in the pit of my soul urges me not to. I can't lie. Not about that. If this Calling of mine is going to be successful at any level, it will be on my terms. It's a matter of me figuring out the best angle possible, and after hearing the thinly veiled lies of Revalia, I refuse to partake in the same game. "Nothing," I say. "Nothing happened, I swear."

She gives a quick nod, as if to thank me for my honesty, as if to say she believed I was being truthful. "Just stay away from him, okay?" she barks before turning on her heel and heading back to her tent.

Chapter Thirteen

Bright Angel Phantom Ranch

I'm up at daybreak the next morning to the sounds of the Canyon and the campers springing to life in rhythmic succession. One by one, bird chirp by bird chirp, voice by voice, tent zipper by tent zipper, the sounds merge to form the glorious song of the morn. Up and at 'em, time to start the day. Malek is one step ahead of me, as he's packed up most of our gear.

Steve is talking to some of the others as they're packing up their gear and drinking their last sips of water from their canteens before refilling their supplies. His voice echoes in the woodlands with a boisterous sense of pride and overwhelming love of this terrain. It's almost as if he's one with the Canyon—comfortable, home. He's doling out last-minute reminders and cautions—admonishing us to be wary of the various forms of wildlife whether they are dangerous or not. Everything in the natural scope of the Canyon has its place and should be left undisturbed. Janice whines about wanting to take pictures of the wildlife for her scrapbook, and Steve laughs at her. "Sweetie," he says, "Bright Angel Trail is a tough one—easy to go down but extremely rough to go back up. I highly recommend paying attention to where you're going and what you're doing rather than snapping some photographs. You'll

have plenty of time for all that sightseeing once we get to Phantom Ranch." Janice mutters something I don't understand, and I figure it's about time for me to get myself in gear.

I stretch out, stand up, and exit my tent only to be startled by Malek standing outside the opening. "Jeez!" I say as my body tenses in shock.

He laughs. "Was about to wake you up. On the jumpy side, aren't we?"

I playfully punch his shoulder. "No! Just don't go sneaking up on me like that anymore!"

"Oh, I won't! Wouldn't want you plunging over the side of Bright Angel Trail." He winks at me. It's a peculiar gesture to accompany such a macabre statement. Usually, there's a double or hidden meaning behind Malek's words, and this time is no exception. I get the feeling he's giving me a hint or a pointer or a *push* in the right direction. Well, his version of the right direction, anyway. He thinks he's so clever sometimes...

Once any trace of our group has been wiped away at the Mather Campground, Tara motions her arms in giant circles, beckoning us to join her for what seems to be our one final pep-talk before we descend into the Canyon. Everyone seems to be ready and excited to get going on our adventure. Janice hangs on to Dylan's shoulder and is practically jumping up and down like a child about to go on a dangerous roller-coaster. Revalia and Lozhure have their packs on their backs and stand together. Only once does she glance in my direction, but quickly looks away when I return her stare. Scott and Jess are next to each other but could as well be miles apart. They don't speak, or touch, or interact, and I assume the wounds are still fresh from their argument last night.

"Okay, Wild Westers!" Tara exclaims as everyone pulls closer to her. "Like Steve said before, Bright Angel Trail is a doozy. Don't be deceived by her glorious beauty. Enjoy it, but don't get too comfortable with it. You're gonna think it an easy trek as we go down. The ten miles to Phantom Ranch will take us a good five to six hours. There are three rest stations, and Steve and I have allotted thirty minutes at each. The pace down will be brisk, but like I said, enjoy it now because trekking back up is a whole other animal! Alright, folks! Let's head on out!"

The group claps and cheers, and we all follow behind Steve and Tara in almost a single file line.

"So!" Steve begins, shouting down the line, "The Bright Angel Trail is considered the park's premier hiking trail. Early pioneers first built a trail in 1891 to reach mining sites below the rim. The pioneers then registered their trail as a toll road and extended the trail to the river.

But in 1928, the trail was turned over to the National Park Service. It's no doubt Bright Angel Trail has a rich history of..."

I tune Steve out and reflect on this act of hiking. The name alone makes me giggle—*Bright Angel Trail*. I have something for Steve to add to the history of it all! I bet this is the first time Bright Angel Trail has seen angels on it! If only those early pioneers could see us now— two angels made flesh, one demon in disguise, and one... who even knows what I've become at this moment in time! I laugh out loud, and Malek swats his canteen strap at my arm to get my attention. "Nothing, nothing," I say, waving my hand in the air.

I think about our destination, and it's as if this little place in the universe is speaking directly to me. *Phantom Ranch*. That's our end-point. End game? The ominously named *Phantom Ranch* doesn't make me giggle or laugh out loud like *Bright Angel Trail* did because for the others in my group, it really is just a name, but for me, it means so much more. What steps will I have to take to meet my goal? I try not to think about it as I walk along the trail. Instead, I take Tara's advice and enjoy the glorious scenery around me.

—x–x※x–x—

The hike took a little less than six hours, like our guides had predicted. Nothing major happened along the way, except for Janice constantly complaining about the heat or whining about her pack being too heavy. Poor Dylan was exhausted by the time we reached our cabins at Phantom Ranch—physically and mentally!

We all settled into our cabins at the Ranch—each one a small, stone structure trimmed with a dark green door and shutters lined in a row one next to the other. Each "couple" has their own space, and this leg of the trip is to last three nights. When we arrived, Malek had claimed the top portion of the bunk bed before whisking off to the dormitory for dinner with a bunch of the others. I have no interest in going there yet. Revalia had mentioned her Watcher being one of the head people at the Ranch, and I don't feel up to the confrontation, so I lazily begin unpacking my stuff.

Screams ring out from the cabin next to mine, and I drop my pack to the wooden floor. Like a wild animal, my ears perk up trying to decipher the sound, voice, and distress level. Another scream, and I'm certain

it's Jess in trouble. I stop everything and race over to her dorm to see what's going on.

I barge through the door, and she screams again in terror. I find her huddled in a corner of the small room with her arms shielding her face. "What's wrong? What's wrong?" I yell over her terrified cries.

"Aestra? Don't come in!" she shrieks. "There's a snake in here!"

My body tenses, and I frantically survey the room. "Where? Where? I don't see one!"

Her arm juts out. "The bed! It's on the bed!"

I look at the bed, which is about three feet in front of me, and see nothing but a pile of clothes strewn out across it. My muscles relax and I take a step forward. "Jess! You're being paranoid!" I sigh. "It's just a pile of..."

Rattling.

A whimper escapes Jess's mouth, and the tiny hairs on my forearms stand at attention. I freeze in my tracks and stare at the bed. The rattle sound goes off once more as the creature rears its head from a chestnut brown piece of clothing. I'm paralyzed, unable to move, as it arches its neck in full view and rattles its warning signal at me again.

"Oh God, oh God, oh God!" Jess mumbles in the corner.

"Just don't move!" I command. But my insides are shaking, and my heart is pounding so hard I can feel it thumping against my rib cage.

"Where is everyone," I whisper from the corner of my mouth.

"The...the..." she stammers.

"If you don't breathe, you're gonna pass out!" I admonish.

"Okay, okay," she says as I hear her taking deep breaths. "They're all at the dining hall. Oh God, Aestra! What are we gonna..."

The snake shakes its tail once more, silencing Jess.

"Just relax," I say in a calm voice. "We'll figure this out. Don't you remember what Steve said on the trail before? This little guy's not gonna go all crazy on us and strike. He rattles at us to warn us."

The snake moves his head back and forth as if he's surveying me, sizing me up, wondering if I am a threat or if I'm something more, like a snack or a meal.

"Remember," I continue, "they don't want to waste their venom on something they can't eat. So do you think he's gonna eat us?"

She nervously laughs in the corner. "No. But there's only one way for him to get out and you're in front of it! How are we gonna usher out a rattlesnake *without* getting bitten!"

I look over to Jess. She's balled up in the corner with her face in her hands. "Just stay where you are," I say.

"Trust me, I ain't going anywhere!" she says, her voice muffled in her hands.

I stare at the snake—stare at his eyes—the two yellow slats stand out against his mottled pattern of dark and light browns. His head moves back and forth as if he's giving me an extra warning, as if he's telling me he will strike me down at any given moment. Ideally, he would let me step aside to Jess in the corner, slither himself off the bed, and out the door calmly and peacefully. No one would have to get hurt, and we all go about our merry way. But that's not in the plan. He feels threatened by not one, but two larger, unfamiliar creatures, and the rattling of his tail lets me know he won't leave here without a fight.

I hate to admit it, but he's beautiful, and his back-and-forth movement almost enthralls me. The way the scales on his underbelly glisten and ripple when he moves up and down is enough to make me put my guard down and observe this interesting life form. The Creator surely used some creativity when forming these things! I find myself more entranced than afraid, like how Eve must have felt when The Morning Star sneaked up on her in the Garden.

And then it hits me. Lucifer favored the shape of the snake because of its dynamic construction, ease of motion, and fearsome visage. For him to have taken on their form, he had to have tamed them—charmed them—in some way so they would bow to his will.

I know I must act quickly before I am hypnotized any further by the creature. "Jessica!" I say with a firm voice. "I have an idea. But I need you to stay still. Just stay huddled the way you are, keep your eyes closed, and whatever you do, don't look up."

"Why?" she whimpers. "What are you gonna do?"

"Just trust me, please. I think I can get it out of here."

"Oh, God! You're gonna kill it, aren't you?"

"That's not my immediate plan, but if I have to chop its…"

She squeals in terror and grabs the sides of her arms tightly as her head is nuzzled between her chest and thighs. "Okay! Okay! Just… just tell me when it's over!"

I reach up, remove my medallion from my neck, and hold it out at my side. The snake's rattling gets deeper, louder, and more intense, as if my movement is a direct challenge to his warnings.

I breathe in as the dark magic swirls around me like a black cloud, shifting in a maelstrom around my body. I pause for a second then I let the medallion fall to the floor, lifting the invisible cloak from my body and revealing my true form. I extend my wings at my side, shaking them from their hidden void, and continue to stare down the animal. As if knowing who I am, the snake lowers its head—kowtowing to my otherworldly presence—and he tones his rattling down to a submissive, nearly inaudible hum. A powerful sensation overcomes me, and I stand tall in my true form. Mine is *not* a body of weakness, that's for sure! The snake quivers before me, like all beings would if they saw my genuine shape!

I take a step to the side, shake my wings one last time, and motion my hand to the opened door. The snake slowly slithers off the bed and takes his leave of the cabin.

Once he's gone, I breathe a sigh of relief, but then quickly scoop the medallion, creating my mask once more. "Gone!" I say, and Jess slowly peers her head from her hands.

"Did you...?"

"No. I didn't have to kill it," I answer.

She stands and walks over to me, throwing her arms around me in a frantic embrace. "Oh, God! I thought I was gonna die!" she says as she begins crying hot tears in the crook of my neck.

I pat her back. "Hey! Hey! It's okay," I try to coax. "I got rid of that silly thing. No one's gonna get dead!"

Through her tears of fear, and relief, and frustration, she snorts and releases me. "I wish it had been Scott trapped in here!" she says with a laugh. To the human ear, it's a joke—a dig at her absent and troubled lover, but to my ears, I hear much more beneath the words.

"You okay?" I ask.

She snorts again through her tears. "Yeah. Yeah. I guess so. I just..." she throws her body onto the bed and buries her face in the unsorted clothes. "This was supposed to be our special time together, and he goes and ruins everything. I don't even know why I stay with him anymore."

"Why? What did he do?" I pry.

She pops her head up from the clothes on the bed. Her eyes are red and swollen from the ordeal of the afternoon and the stress from her situation. They go wild as the memories of every wrong Scott has done to her come crashing into the front of her mind. "Well, where do I start? He loves his job. Puts it above everything else. Loves making money, and spending money, and saving money, and investing money. Money, money, money. That's his Queen. He makes promises he doesn't keep. We were supposed to get engaged after high school. Then college. Now it's not until he's saved enough money. See where I'm going with this? And I know he's cheated on me. Found that one out the hard way!"

She stops to take a breath, and I don't know what to say or how to respond to any of this. "It'll be okay," I say, and immediately wish I could take it back.

She pauses and looks at me like *I'm* the crazy one, but then her face softens and more tears stream down her face. "I'm sorry," she gushes. "You don't even know me, and you save my life from a freaking rattlesnake, and now I'm unleashing all my problems on you."

"No worries. I understand how relationships can be," I lie, because really? What experience do I have with relationships? How am I equipped to even offer this poor, pathetic girl any stitch of advice on how to handle her failing relationship? The only relationship I'm trying to repair is the one with my Father, and I'm not exactly in the plus column on that one.

Jess wipes her eyes with the back of her hand. "Yeah. I guess so. Comes with the female territory, I suppose." She forces a smile. "It sucks they make us feel crazy sometimes! Sometimes, I swear I would be better off without him. Like, I'd be better off if he were dead!"

I sit on the bed next to her. "Oh, you don't mean that," I say, but my words are lightly salted in sarcasm.

She laughs. "Oh, Aestra! Sometimes I wish I didn't mean it. The thought has crossed my mind, to be honest with you. And being out here... in the Canyon. Would be *easy* to have an accident!" Once again, I detect a sinister seriousness behind her playful tone.

"Oh, come on!" I scoff, trying to diminish the severity of her words.

She chuckles again. "Oh, come on, nothing! Don't tell me you never had a guy problem that was so bad that the thought of 'getting rid of him' didn't cross your mind."

No. I don't know. I've never had that feeling or that experience. This much, I can't relate to. "I don't know," I ultimately say. "But I sure do understand your frustration."

She moves closer to me on the bed and puts her head on my shoulder. "Thanks for everything," she coos in my ear. "Thanks for saving my ass from that snake, and thanks for listening to me go off like that. I'm sorry if I was such a bitch to you before."

I wrap my arm around her back and bring my hand up to touch her hair. "We girls gotta stick together," I say, and it sounds like a 'girl-power' rally cry.

"We sure do," she replies.

She repositions herself closer to me and curls her knees onto my lap like a little sister finding comfort in her sibling. My medallion brushes against the outline of her chest, and I suddenly feel a rush of calming power descend over the both of us. It's as if she's penetrated through the outer shell of my veneer and is now entwined within my magic. The magnetic field pulsates around us, surrounding our bodies and drenching us in its powerful hold. Her body droops a little against mine. I know her human form is being lulled into a cosmic trance, and a darkness inside of me sees an opening unlike any other.

You do what you gotta do, I think. *I wouldn't blame you for it.*

She nuzzles her face against my cheek and whispers, "Thank you" in my ear.

CHAPTER FOURTEEN

WATCHER

I'm not keeping up with my "story" very well because the others all went out on their rafting excursion today, and I opted to stay behind. If it were a problem, though, I think Malek would have indicated so, yet there were no protests from him when I said I wasn't going. He smiled, waved, and went jogging along to catch up with the rest of them. If anyone would have any indication of how this grand tragedy is supposed to play out, it would be Malek, so if he's okay with me not being too much of a thrill seeker today, then so am I.

There are water faucets for hose hookups attached to the side of each little cabin here in Phantom Ranch. I turn mine on and let the water cleanse my dusty feet. The pressure is weak, but that's to be expected in the heart of the Canyon, and the water spits out blazing hot at first, then calms to a cold stream. It feels good to wash away the mesa from my skin—the orange dust coagulates to a light brown, dirt substance between my toes and runs over the sides of my sandals. Tara and Steve had advised all of us to wear sneakers at all times, but every once in a while I slip on my sandals so I can feel the actual earth underneath me. The humans often take for granted the wonders of their own world, making afterthoughts of something as simple as dirt particles.

But for me... for someone who has danced amongst the clouds and only dreamed of feeling ground against the soles of my feet—this moment is like a dream come true for me. Yet, I suppose it isn't much different from the human wants and desires, for theirs mirror the exact opposite of mine—they dream of heavenly wings and paradise and God.

The grass always seems greener...

Or, in my case, oranger.

"Aestra?" a voice calls.

I look to see Revalia's face peering from behind my cabin, her body hidden by the stone wall. A few strands of her brown hair stick to her temples with sweat while others wildly frame her face, untamed from the morning humidity.

"What?" I say sharply.

She reveals the rest of her body and comes into my full view. She looks worried, tired. Perhaps she's worried she will not succeed in her Calling... again. I wonder what punishment she would endure for that one, if there was a punishment at all. Who knows how the Creator operates or does what He does, because everything kinda seems so arbitrary at this point.

Revalia walks toward me, and I shut off the valve of the water spigot. "I want you to meet someone," she says.

Her Watcher.

"I don't know," I say. "I'm not sure that's..."

In an instant hot breath is on my neck, and before I can swivel my body to face who is behind me, someone grabs both my arms and pins them against my back. "Not really up for debate," a voice whispers in my ear.

Lozhure.

My face burns with rage, and I buck my body wildly against his hold, fighting to get free. It's a familiar hold, too, because he's done this to me before. I know him all too well—the sound of his voice whispering in my ear, the touch of his hands squeezing my wrists tightly into place. He had restrained me against my will in The Observatory, and I begged him to stop, begged him to let me go. Even though he hadn't, I still forgave him for violating me, for forcing me into a position I was not comfortable with.

But this time is different.

This time I will continue to fight against him, and not beg to be freed.

And this time, I will not forgive.

I kick at him from behind, scream at them, curse at them. Revalia looks at me with a pained expression, as if to say she's sorry. But she's not sorry. She has a mission to accomplish like I do, and it's obvious to me, she's willing to do whatever it takes to make her trip to Earth a successful one.

With his free hand, Lozhure covers my mouth with a ragged piece of cloth. It smells sweet—so sweet it almost gags me. Before I can rear forward and smash his forehead with the back of my skull, everything goes fuzzy and black.

I wake up to the sound of a door lock clicking shut. My stomach aches a little and my eyes flutter into focus. I'm lying on a couch in the back room of the general office while Revalia and Lozhure stand in front of me. A tall woman with short blonde hair stands next to a wooden desk behind them.

"She's awake!" Lozhure calls out, and the woman hurries over to me.

As the woman draws near, I hear a buzzing sound like a hundred bees swarming in the room. I quickly look around, trying to locate the source of the sound, but she smiles softly at me.

"Aestra, this is our Watcher, Ruth Sterling," Revalia says.

Ruth Sterling.

The name sounds familiar to my ears, but I can't put my finger on how I would know it. She stands in front of me, and I notice she has a silver pulsating aura around her, indicating to me she is not human— not fully, at least. She is a Watcher, one of the Nephilim: one of the children of the fallen angels and the human women. Born of this Earth but connected to the Creator unlike any other. She is the by-product of the unnatural union of angelic and human essences. And although she is heavily shrouded in magic to conceal her identity, my ethereal essence is able to glean bits and pieces of her true visage.

"I know you," I say to her with a hoarse voice.

Revalia gasps, and the woman pulls back a little, her hand darting to her chest in surprise. "What do you mean, you remember me? What do you remember? Tell me what you know," she says, almost panicked.

"I know you," I repeat. "You're one of the women from the picture I saw. When I was in Asphodel. There was a house. A room. A teenage girl's room. There were pictures. You were in them." I'm sure I'm not making much sense because Lozhure and Revalia look confused at what I say, and I'm still a little groggy from whatever sedative Lozhure used to knock me out.

The woman relaxes her hand and the muscles in her face, understanding my drivel. "That version no longer exists."

I rub my temples and sit up on the couch. I direct a hateful gaze to Lozhure. "So, this is what He sends you to do, right?" I practically spit at him. "You and Revalia play good guy bad guy? When her sweet strategies don't work, you step in as the thug? The muscle?" He doesn't look at me. He can't. He's too ashamed. I look to Revalia. "I guess when you've already failed once, you gotta do what you gotta do, right?" A lump forms in her throat with a croaking sound. "The two of you are no better than Lucifer's underlings, you know that? I wonder if Camael knows the tactics you two are using in your..."

Ruth sits on the couch next to me. "Easy, Aestra. No one is here to attack you or bully you. We're all here because we care about you very much, and we want what's best for you, that's all."

Ah! A little angelic intervention.

I shake my head. "Well, I think *Logan* here already crossed that line by drugging me and dragging me over here."

Revalia shudders at my words. "We had no other choice, Aestra!" she pleads. "You weren't going to come talk to us on your own."

"But that's not for you to decide!" I bark back. "That's for me to decide. Not for you to force on me. Is this how you behave on all your Callings?" I stand and start to walk to the door, but Revalia reaches her hand out to stop me. I jerk my arm out from her hand. "Don't touch me! I can't believe you did this to me! I can't believe you let *him*," I point my finger like a gun at Lozhure, "do that to me again too!"

She lowers her head, speechless, as Ruth waves her hand in the air. "Revalia. Lozhure," she says calmly, "maybe it would be best if I spoke to Aestra alone."

The two look at Ruth, then at each other one last time before they turn around and walk out the door. I rub my sweaty hands down the sides of my shorts as Ruth rises from the couch to meet me. I can't deny the intensity of her presence, because aside from Malek, she is the only other immortal I have come into contact with since I've been on Earth.

She looks me up and down, scanning my face, taking in the shape and structure of my body, fixing her eyes on my medallion. "I know you too," she says. Her voice is sweet like honey—warm, amber, raw in the hive. She narrows her eyes sympathetically, like she knows a secret, but can't tell me.

"How could you? I..."

"I know there's much you don't remember, but you and I go way back," she gives a small, apologetic smile. "I'm sorry if I failed you in any way, Aestra, but I'm here now, and I want to help you however I can."

How did she fail me? I've never seen this woman in my entire life, except in that picture, and she's sorry for failing me?

"I know how confused you must feel," she begins. Perhaps the expression on my face gave that away. I have to remember to work on not letting my feelings show too much! "But I understand what you're going through. I've seen many conflicted angels at a crossroads in their path. I know how fiercely you love humankind, and it's natural for your kind to feel that way! I've been the Watcher to many an angel who has had a deep affinity toward the Lord's creation." She reaches for my hands, holds them out in the space between us, and looks deeply into my eyes. "And I know how much you've sacrificed, and all the awful deeds you've done because of that love."

"What sacrifices? What awful deeds?"

"You know I can't tell you, Aestra. But know this—because of your love, oceans raged at your command."

She's lost me. Utterly and completely lost me. In my frustration, I pull away from her grasp and turn for the door. "I don't know what you're talking about. I don't remember you or anything you're saying. I don't know how you think you can help me."

"Listen to me," she calls out. "If you appear to me in your true form, there is a chance you could have a spark of memory."

I hold up my medallion away from my chest. "This?"

She nods. "It's not like Revalia and Lozhure who are fully human right now. They can't see me or have any ethereal notions. You are not changed, only glamoured. You are shrouded by the same spell that hides my true figure from the world. Remove the necklace, and not only will I be able to see you as you truly are, but you will be able to see me as well. And that might bring something back to you. That is how I can help."

I remove the chain from my neck and dangle the pendant in the air. I give her one last warning before I let it go. "You called me an angel. I'll have you know, angel I am not. I'm not anything, at least not yet."

"I fear not your transformation," she says melodically, like a long-forgotten song of the ancients.

I drop the chain and am nearly blinded by a silver light the second it hits the floor. Without the magic attached to the charm, I see Ruth

before me in all her Nephilim beauty. She is giant, massive, God-like. Her silver glow fills the room not only with a piercing light but also with a buzzing sound. There is a swarm of bees at her feet, encircling her, moving and gliding with her, flitting about her at her giantess command. The buzzing song makes me sway back and forth as I try to scan her, try to open my transcendent floodgates and tap into hers.

She doesn't flinch when she sees me—black wings, horns, and misshapen feet. In fact, she smiles in the way a mother would smile at seeing their disfigured child after an accident. Like there is love still... a bittersweet love because your darling no longer looks the same.

I had an accident once.

My wings were ripped from my astral bones.

My parents were killed.

The bees wrapped me in a blanket and tried to protect me. Tried to help me.

My hands bled onto desert sand in the shadows of the colossal ancient structures, and I tried to dry them on my feathers, only to be slashed with razors.

"We are sisters, you and I," she sings with her deep, honey voice. "Immortal wanderers—aberrations, if you will."

I swoop down and pick up the medallion, cloaking us both within the confines of our spells. The last specks of silver flicker around her, disintegrating into speckled dust flakes. The buzzing of the bees fades to an inaudible decibel. "Immortal," I repeat.

She nods. "I know no death, Aestra. Same as you."

"So, Earth... this place, this realm, this dwelling. This is your Hell?"

"Why would you say that?" she asks, seemingly bothered by my question.

"You can never be in the presence of the Creator if you can never die. That is Hell, isn't it?"

"No, Aestra. The Creator is with me always. He's in my heart and in my mind. I believe in Him and have faith He is the true light and the way. He is the Redeemer. The Judge. But He also shows His kindness and mercy."

Such a human response. *Pre-programmed,* as Malek would say. "Listen, I have one objective, and one objective only—get back to Ilarium and find out what happened to me," I say curtly.

She closes her blue eyes for a second and nods her head. "You didn't have any memories before?"

"No," I lie. I don't want to tell her what I saw and felt because it doesn't make sense to me, and I know I'll be met with more riddles and jargon.

"Aestra, I am the conduit. I am the direct connection to Ilarium. I can help you. The Lord will shower you in His mercy if you are sorry for what you have done. He will not ask any questions. He will welcome you back to Ilarium with open arms."

Revalia explained all this to me. And I stand firm in how I feel—how can I seek forgiveness when I don't even know what I'm asking forgiveness for?

I move closer to the door, my back turned to Ruth. "Do you dream of Ilarium?" I ask.

"Of course, I do!" she exclaims, almost breathlessly.

"So, what about your soul? If you're immortal, you'll never die. If you never die, your soul will never be able to feel the joys of Ilarium. Heavenly paradise. The reward for your service to the Creator."

I turn my head over my shoulder to see the expression on her face. She is steadfast, unwavering in her convictions. "I am all soul and have none at the same time. Those like me, other Watchers, we are content with the bargain our angel and mortal parents made with the Creator. We are content with our eternal arrangement."

The word "bargain" makes me think back to what Revalia said to me the other day: *And even though you walk among the demons, Aestra, the Lord will forgive you. For His love is all powerful and all-encompassing and demands no bargain in return.*

The memory of her words strikes me deeply, and I walk out of the office without saying another word. I have made up my mind. I am alone in this. I will get the answers I seek, even if it means doing the unthinkable—what's good for them, should be good for me. If they can easily drug and kidnap and bully and push around others to get their way, I can insinuate a little homicide, right? I will break the shackles that bind me to Asphodel and find my way back to Ilarium, on my own terms. If all it takes is a heartfelt apology, then I'll do what needs to be done now, and beg forgiveness later.

All is not as it seems. I will no longer be influenced or swayed or taken hostage by anyone else.

-PART III-
THE FALLOUT

estranged—*to turn away in feeling or affection; make unfriendly or hostile; alienate the affections of; replacement of love and belonging with apathy and hostility.*

SNAKES ON THE TRAIL

I've traveled close to ten miles into the heart of the Canyon, and as I sit by myself in a secluded area away from the cabins, dining hall, and dormitories, I look up above at the canyon cliffs that surround me. I am insignificant in this grand scheme of pulsating life. Just another vehicle to emit carbon dioxide and feed the machine we call Earth. I am small amongst these rocky walls. They encase me in their primal grip, enclose me in their stony fingers. No wonder the humans have such mixed emotions about themselves, about their faith, about their position in the world. As an angel flitting about Ilarium, I was able to see *over* them all—all at once from a higher perspective. But now, here, at the ominously named Phantom Ranch where I am below the precipice of an ancient monolith, the perspective is much, much different.

There is much to absorb, and I don't mean the scenery. That, too, comes with its own merit of wonder and awe, but the main issue I must reflect upon is what seems like a struggle for my attention, for my affection, for my service—*for my soul*. The external forces are stating their strong cases. Both Revalia's side and Malek's side have clear positions and intentions, and I am certainly being pulled in both directions. But there is also the internal force that screams for answers. Me.

My soul. My sanity. I crave the knowledge of my past actions and the comfort of the joys of Ilarium, yet I crave the independence only Malek can give. In times of doubt or confusion, I would always pray on it. And I realize, since I was deposited in Asphodel, I have not prayed. Sure, I begged, pleaded, cried, wailed in fear and agony, but I have not *prayed*. I have not said a thoughtful or heartfelt prayer. That's another concept most humans don't understand—not all prayers are requests. And I have been guilty of that myself. I have been demanding answers, screaming my desires and wishes, treating the Creator as if he were some long bearded man on a sleigh granting wishes to the children of the world. Yes, I am His child, but prayer doesn't work like that all the time. Actually, a lot of the time, prayer is more about listening than it is about speaking.

So, I do just that—I listen. I close my eyes, set my hands behind me in the orange dust and dirt, feeling every scratchy granule against my fingers, and I prop the weight of my body against my arms at an angle. I tune out all the sounds of the Canyon until I hear nothing but the swooshing silence in my ears. A wave of energy rushes from my stomach and into my chest and I let myself go. I am at peace, calm and open. I speak from my heart and listen with my preternatural ears:

Lord, I know I have begged and pleaded with You looking for some kind of answers—for some kind of salvation. Now I realize to make restitution I must be truly sorry for the things I have done, but I am struggling, Father. I am struggling to feel sorrow when I don't know what I am supposed to be sorry for. I am in the dark. I am blinded by a seductive power and a doubt that has cast its shadow over my heart. I come to You now, not looking for an explanation, but to give to You what feels like my last sliver of Ilarium. You know how much I have cherished Your creations, Almighty One. You know how much I love Your grand design. Oh, Heavenly Father, Camael once told me I was most beloved, that I was most special. And now, I feel I have been reduced to nothing more than the orange ash I sit upon. If this be Your will, I accept the road ahead of me, but I am fighting against the Now and the Here, Lord. And in my complete confusion, I turn to You. I offer to You not my apology, but my devotion and dedication, as I have never swayed in my intentions to You. This, I pray.

I pause, taking in the silence around me, reflecting on my words, syncopating my breathing to the pulsing heartbeat of the world—the ebb and flow of my natural surroundings. An energy rises and falls in my chest with every deep breath I take, and I have completely given myself over to the higher power of the Lord.

I wait for a sign, for an inkling of a response. Of something. Anything.

I suck in one last breath of canyon air, my chest rising to full capacity, and I hold it there, opening myself to any kind of shift in the atmosphere that would indicate an acknowledgement only my instincts could tap into.

I pause.

I hold.

I wait.

And I am met with nothing but silence—a silence that chills me in this warm domain. It is a silence that is more than just the absence of my Father—it is a sign, a clear and deafening one at that. My heart drops a little. I didn't know what to expect from my prayer, but this was surely not the response I had prepared myself for. I reached out to the Lord with the last sheen of Ilarium I had left in me, only to have it dissipate to oblivion and leave me as an abandoned child of a vengeful god.

I slowly open my eyes, ready to look at the world through my orphan lenses, and that's when I notice them. *Them.* A slithering mass of rattles and hums meandering in the dust and dirt, whipping their tails in rhythmic time. There must be thirty or forty of them, and all are coiled with their rattler shaking in their body loop and their necks arched at attention. As I eye each one, it lowers its head as if it were genuflecting, bowing before me.

I remain calm and still as, one by one, the Western Diamondbacks approach me. I feel no fear as they surround me in a circle, rattling their song of praise and worship. They acknowledge the growing essence of darkness within my soul like a butterfly with black wings trapped in its cocoon. Can they see my wings? Can their reptile eyes see beyond my medallion veneer? Can they see *me* in all my monstrous glory? And one by one, they slither at my feet and across my legs, wriggling their silky bodies and twisting themselves up my arms and across the backs of my shoulders. Their rattle song is not one of warning but one of acceptance. They will not harm me. Their flicking tongues pelt my skin, speaking to me a lullaby, a story, a memory...

Beneath the rhythm of their song, I remember.

I've lived this human life before, except I wasn't glamoured the way I am now. I was human. I was real. Like how Revalia and Lozhure transformed. I remember the fabricated memories forced together with my

angel essence. I remember pain and suffering—the agonies of a child witnessing the death of her life-givers. I remember the desecration of my wings—plumes of white feathers slipping from my grasp as I fell from the energy source in Ilarium. They tore away piece by piece from my fused human spinal column as I transformed from astral matter, to simulated human guise, to actual flesh and bone. I remember the pain as I fell. I remember pain as I hit the cold earth and as the memories of my human persona flooded my existence. I remember confusion upon seeing Ruth Sterling—*Aunt Ruth*—for the first time. She was my Watcher back then. My Watcher who had a quaint brownstone in New York City. My Watcher who was the sister of my dead human mother. My Watcher who was assigned to me to guide me on my Calling. Only, I don't remember my Calling or any of the details about it. I scan my mind, and try as I might, there are no recollections. No memories. No sparks. I can't even recall if I was successful or not. Yet, there's something else that comes to me as the snakes continue to hiss in my ears. I remember someone else from my time as a human.

I remember Malek.

I remember Malek and his stormy eyes and a pretty pendant he gave me—forged for me. I remember sitting on a bed with him at a party and discussing the amulet and its power and my intentions with my Calling. I remember spending mornings at a diner with him pondering the distinctions between human and angel and demon beings. And I remember him being with me in a park before I went back to Ilarium, telling me it was going to be okay, telling me I did an excellent job.

I turn my head from the snakes that have now covered my entire body, and Malek is standing beside me. His eyes are slightly wider than usual, and I assume he's taken aback by my slithering adornment.

"Enough!" I say to the rattlers, and in an instant, they leave me and slink back to the canyon.

I stand and face him, and there's something different in his eyes. A distinctive look. An unusual color. Perhaps he's reflecting the expression on my own face, from my own eyes, because there's an unspoken hint of *knowing* between us. He smiles, and I know he knows that *I* know. He knows I've remembered something.

He sighs, and I can't tell if it's a sigh of relief, happiness, or a little of both. "There's my Morning Glory," he says, and the words ignite more clicks, more sparks of memory in my mind.

I take both of his hands in mine. "It's not all back," I say.

He brings our hands between our chests, so our medallions are touching our forearms. "I didn't expect it to be."

"Did I fail?" I whisper. "Did I fail in my Calling?"

He raises his eyebrows and inches closer to me. "By whose standards?"

"Anyone's," I answer.

"Success and failure are both predicated on perception, Aestrangel. You above anyone should be aware of that."

He smiles at me with his eyes—his gentle, loving eyes. Gray, blue, and green, frothing with the seafoam of the ocean. I can hear the waves crashing in his eyes and feel the crunchy sand between my toes. I can't deny that since my journey began, Malek Forcas has been the one stable constant in my life.

"I'm sorry I had forgotten you," I say.

He smiles wider, "I knew you'd remember in time."

I stare at him long and hard, scanning his face, like I am rediscovering an old friend after a long separation. *My* old friend—the only one I have right now, and quite possibly the only one I've ever had.

It seems like forever that we gaze into each other's eyes. I wonder what he sees when he looks at me. Does *he* see a friend in me? Does he see me as an obligation to his father? Does he see me as an opportunity to advance his ranking?

"Stop thinking so loud," he laughs.

Before I get a chance to protest, he lets go of my hands and raises my chin. He bends slightly and kisses me on the lips. Deep and passionate. His electricity races through my face and neck, down my arms and torso and lower body. The power surge hurts and yet feels invigorating at the same time. I lose myself in his kiss, in the ocean, in the moment. Our mouths move relentlessly over each other—arms entangled around black-outlined bodies, tongues dancing like snakes sensing the heat of their prey, lips bitten and pulled, faces nearly swallowed in a rush of high voltage ecstasy. I am whole in this moment. I am safe. I am complete. Like a fulfilled essence. Like an answered prayer.

"Aestra! No!" a voice screeches in the valley, violently pulling Malek and me out of our moment.

I look to see Revalia a few feet away. A look of horror is plastered on her face.

She runs toward us. "I've been looking all over for you!" she yells. She looks at me and then to Malek. Her face twists in horror and disgust

when she registers that, yes, he and I were in the midst of some strange and dark passionate kiss. She stomps her foot on the ground like an insolent child, "You can't do this, Aestra! You know what he is!"

I bite my bottom lip to suppress the rush of anger swelling inside of me. I look at Revalia, then to Malek, and then back to her. How dare she? I feel nothing but contempt and resentment toward her right now! What makes her think she can waltz into my situation and call the shots? And for what? Our Father, who art in Ilarium? "Do *you* know what *I* am?" I challenge behind clenched teeth.

"Yes! Yes, Aestra! You are a child of God. You are a child of God chosen for greatness."

"That's right," Malek interrupts. "She is a child of your god, but she was chosen by The Morning Star for a purpose grander than your Creator."

Revalia spits on the ground, her saliva mixing with the dirt and forming a little dirty pool at her feet. "Don't you dare speak to me, demon!"

Without thinking, I grab Malek's hand and intertwine our fingers in a show of solidarity and defiance. Revalia silently gasps, and her eyes go wild with disbelief.

"We're all family here," Malek says with his usual Malek charm.

But Revalia ignores him and speaks directly to me. "Aestra! You're my best friend. My sister. Please. I can help you." She puts out her hands in a surrendering gesture. "I can help you see the way. Pray with me. We can both pray for forgiveness together, and our Father will light the path for us to get home."

But I've already prayed, Revalia, and our Father is not listening.

She makes a motion to step forward, but a rattling noise fills the valley. A rattle and a hiss. Collectively, the snakes come out of hiding and start to make their way around Malek and me. Their rattle song is now a warning. Revalia recognizes the threat and takes a cautious step back.

I lift our intertwined hands. "I'd sooner call him 'brother' before I call you a friend."

Tears start to pool in her eyes. "Don't say these things, Aestra! Your words make me feel like an overturned boat in a river, and I can't escape. Your words make me feel as if I'm free-falling without a parachute! How did we ever get to this point? How can we turn back the hands of time?"

"There are no hands," I say matter-of-factly. "I've been through the belly of time, and there's no going back for me."

The snakes rattle as if in applause, and Revalia takes another step back.

"Please, just..." she begins, but the snakes' heads rise at attention. Malek stifles a sinister chuckle.

"Not now, Revalia. I don't think you're welcome here."

She relents and walks away.

The snakes go back into hiding, and Malek pulls me in for a dark embrace. I've officially drawn my line in the dirt, and thanks to Revalia, I have some ideas about taking the next steps in my Calling.

CHAPTER SIXTEEN

SEEDS IN THE DESERT

Black clouds hang low in the southern sky. To the north, there is nothing but billowing fluffy clouds set against an azure backdrop. It's as if the world has been divided into darkness and light. Charging from those black clouds, the strange angel makes her way through the impending storm wielding an enormous, blood-stained scythe like the Angel of Death, the Reaper of Souls, the Illuminata. The last word comes into my mind, and I'm not sure why. I haven't heard it before, and yet it's so familiar to me.

The figure dances on the undercurrent of the storm's wind and brandishes her blade in a circular motion as if she is taunting someone. Beneath her, in the valley below, scores of people kneel in prayer with their backs toward her—afraid to look upon her fearsome countenance. I stand among the people, walking among their prayerful rows, watching them cower in terror. The angel turns her blade outward, swoops down from the sky, and begins impaling the kneelers, hooking them on the edge of the scythe. Their spines sever, and their organs spill out onto the ground as they are lifted into the air with her and tossed over her shoulder like trash being discarded. She flies closer and closer, picking the people up, two, sometimes three, at a time. I know she will not come for me. I am safe standing here in the green valley. I can hear my snakes in the distance, and I know I am protected.

When there is one victim left, she hovers slowly, taking her time, savoring the moment before her blade strikes, feeling the power of anticipation bubble inside her. I hear her chuckling behind her mass of black hair. As she rears the scythe back, she pauses and looks at me. The wind picks up, and her hair blows back revealing her true face.

My face.

She smiles at me before slicing her last victim in half.

I jolt awake in a panic nearly punching Malek in the face. My breathing is in labored pants, and it's hard for me to shake the *realness* of the dream off.

Last night, I fell asleep in Malek's arms. I'm not sure exactly how it happened, but at some point during the night, I left my sleeping bag to join him in his. He didn't protest either. I snuggled in his sleeping bag, and he welcomed me with open arms. Our medallions had clanked together when I positioned my body against his, and we both kind of giggled at that. He petted my forehead until I had fallen asleep.

But the dream jarred me, waking him up in the process.

"You okay?" he asks with a groggy voice.

"Yeah, yeah, just a bad dream. But it wasn't a dream. But it was. I... I don't know."

"You wanna talk about it?"

No. I don't want to talk about it. But something about it... the reoccurrence of the dream, the face, the blood... I can't shake it. I can't shake it because it feels too real. It feels like...

Still nestled to his chest, I look at him and catch the light of his gray eyes staring back at me. "Did I... Did I hurt people?" I ask.

He closes his eyes and gives a forward nod.

A cold sensation paralyzes me. I'm almost afraid to ask my next question because deep inside me, deep down in my dark parts, I *know* I know the answer, but that pesky slither of humanness that is in me needs some validation, some confirmation. "I killed people, too, didn't I?"

He breathes in and smiles. A look of pride and pleasure sweeps across his face. "Thousands," he sighs with a perverse ecstasy.

"That's what I thought," I mumble and curl back into him.

He kisses my forehead and says something, but I close my eyes and drift back to sleep.

───✳───

"Okay, Wild Westers! We're all set to get moving up the North Kaibab Trail!" Tara says, rallying everyone together.

Our time at Phantom Ranch has come to an end, and we're on our way to hike back up the Canyon. Steve left early this morning on a mule ride back up Bright Angel Trail. There, he'll get the van and drive over to the North Kaibab Trailhead to pick us up. Part of our "adventure" is the hike back up the North Kaibab Trail, which, according to Tara, the fourteen miles should take us about seven hours or so.

"The NKT is much different than Bright Angel," she adds.

Janice rolls her eyes and throws one of her backpacks into Dylan's arms.

Tara continues explaining. "The hike back up is always a struggle, and this time around there are fewer rest stops before we make it to the Rim. If we have time, we'll explore the Supai Tunnel and Roaring Springs."

Everyone whoops and cheers at this announcement, as it is apparently one of the highlights listed on the initial tour guide pamphlet. I adjust the straps on my pack and pull my black braid over one shoulder. Malek comes from behind me, puts his hand around my hip, and gives me one of his charming, signature winks. It's awkward and weird and strange and creepy and loving and so *wrong* on so many different levels, but I tuck my head in like a crush-eyed teenager and blush. At least, I think I do. No. I know I do because Janice just so happens to turn her head around at that very moment and gives me a look of utter confusion. I can almost hear the thoughts in her head saying in her sickly-sweet Southern drawl, "Ewww, what's *that* about, now?" I smile, which confuses her more.

We start out at a brisk pace, but I know, as the incline gets steeper, we will slow down considerably. In line are Jess, Dylan, Janice, Scott, me, Malek, Revalia, and Lozhure. Tara takes the lead, guiding us through the terrain, regaling us with tales of the seven hundred people who lost their lives in the arms of the Canyon either by their own stupidity or some other more questionable means. "It's amazing to think only 700 people have died here in the Canyon," Tara says in a loud voice so the whole line of us can hear. "With all of the hundreds of people who visit here on a daily basis, the relatively low number of accidents resulting in fatalities is astonishing."

"What about you and Steve?" Janice asks. "Have you guys had any accidents on any of your tours?"

Tara wipes sweat from her forehead. "Nope. We've been lucky. The closest thing we had to a catastrophe was a few years back. One of our Wild Westers decided she was going to go into labor on the Bright Angel Trail. But that's another story for another time."

Everyone laughs, and Tara segues her stories of tragedy into lessons in safety.

About two miles into the hike, we all begin to feel the upward incline of the Canyon. The pace starts to slow just as Tara said it would around this time, but she encourages us to press on. "The first rest stop is right in our reach, and you'll be happy to know that's our official halfway point. We're almost there, guys! Think about it... Steve will be waiting for us at the top of the trail with open arms, cold water, and an air-conditioned van!" More chuckles from the group. Revalia and Lozhure are relatively quiet, though I can feel their eyes boring holes throughout my whole body. They are watching my every move like vultures.

At some point, Janice loses her footing on the slope and falls backward into Scott's arms. I stop in my tracks for a moment so they can get their positioning back on track. She smiles at him, and my senses pick up on something else... something transpires between them—a glance, a smile, an "Oh, I'm sorry," a "Don't worry about it," another smile, a twinkle in the eyes...

Malek had been focused on the trail in front of his feet and walks blindly into me, kicking up a puff of dust at my feet. I snap my head around and scold, "Wanna watch where you're going?" and something transpires between *us*—a glance, a smile, an "Oh, I'm sorry," a twinkle in his eyes. I ignore it and turn back around, pressing forward.

I feel different when I'm around Malek, and I'm not yet able to define the feelings I have for him, for there are so many on so many different conflicting levels. First and foremost, he is an enemy, yet he is the closest thing I have to a best friend. He is a brother—manufactured and, in a way, real. He seems to fulfill a part of me that feels empty—like there's a piece missing inside of me, but when he's around, I feel whole. These feelings are jaded and confused—born from the basic human needs of safety, acceptance, assurance. I trust him, but I don't. I need him, but could do without him. I feel close to him, but reject him for his demonic nature. I hate him, but I love him. At least, I think I love

him. Or rather, I think I hate him. I'm scared those feelings have been blended to be one in the same.

I look back at Revalia and meet her gaze. She gives me a pained look like she's desperately trying to reach me with the power of her mind. Oh, mere mortal, you cannot reach me here! I nod at her, letting her know I understand how hard she is trying, yet I will not give in. She is the furthest thing from my mind right now, and I will call this one early—Revalia has failed. Again.

We reach the Pump House Ranger Station after about four hours of hiking up the trail. Tara tells us we have forty-five minutes to rest, have something to eat, use the facilities, and most importantly, fill our canteens. I find the ladies' restroom next to the watering pump and decide to hide away from them all for a few minutes.

My solace is short-lived. Over the sound of the low-pressure faucet in the women's bathroom, I hear voices whispering outside the little hut. I shut the water off and duck low by the dirty window to get a better sense of what's going on. It's a man and a woman, speaking quietly and quickly. The man's voice is immediately identifiable to me—it's Scott with his empty, soulless timbre. But the woman? She speaks again, and I realize it's Janice's twang. I hold still, listening to the conversation, visualizing the movements of their bodies, putting the twinkle in their eyes from before into a new light.

Their chat starts out innocuously—small talk with a person you have spent a week or so with having the same types of adventures and experiences. But there's a shift in their talk. A pause. An awkward silence. One of them rustles their feet in the dirt. One of them scratches the back of their head. The words between them become staggered. It's a jagged one-word tête-à-tête of meaningless words going back and forth, like a volleyball arching from one opposing side to the other. And then the words stop, replaced by the smacking sounds of mouth against mouth, lips clasping lips.

If only Jess were here to see this.

In my mind's eye, I see Jess walking to the ladies' room, hearing the secret rendezvous, turning to the back of the structure to investigate. Her eyes widening in anger and shock as she stumbles upon her mate in the arms of a married woman. She starts screaming at them, crying, "How could you do this? How could you do this to me?" to which Scott would respond "No, it's not what you think! It's not like that!" And Jess, throwing something against the side of the restroom, curses them both out, and threatens to tell Janice's husband. Janice races away to the rest of the group who are waiting patiently at the picnic tables, as Jess tells Scott to do unspeakable things to himself. Then she would storm into the bathroom and break down in tears on the floor.

Only, there she is.

On the floor. Head in hands. Howling in hurt and anger.

And here I am—crouched low beneath the window like a spy in the night.

Had I willed this? Did I have something to do with Jess's discovery of her cheating partner?

I walk over and bend down beside her, offering my arm as a means of comfort and support. Jess stands immediately from my touch, so I follow her as well. "What are you doing here?" she asks through painful tears.

"I was filling my canteen and..."

"That son of a bitch!" she screams. "I knew it! I knew he was messing around with someone else! Did you see that? Did you see what happened?"

I shake my head sympathetically. "No. But I kinda heard."

"I swear to God, Aestra! I'm done! This is it! This is the last friggin' time he's gonna do this to me!"

All it takes is a tiny little push, a simple suggestion, to propel them in the right direction, so said Malek not so long ago.

I extend my arm to pat her on the back when the door to the bathroom flings open and Revalia bursts in. "Everything okay in here? I heard yelling!"

Jess sniffles, and I take a step forward, positioning my body between Revalia and Jess.

"We're fine," I say. "We'll be fine. I got this, *Reba*. Thanks."

Revalia sidesteps me and stands next to Jess. "Oh, honey. You don't look fine. What happened? Anything I can do to help?"

I glare at Revalia. I want to flare out my wings and wrap them around her body until she can no longer breathe! Here she is, meddling again in my business!

Jess wipes her nose with the back of her hand. "Stupid boyfriend! Or should I say ex-boyfriend!"

"Whatever he's done, I'm sure it's not that bad," Revalia tries to coax.

"Oh, it's bad!" Jess snaps. "It's been bad. I'm over it all, ya know?"

"No relationship comes without its fair share of problems. I'm sure you guys can work this all out."

Jess huffs sarcastically. "*If* he makes it home, I swear, I'm putting all his stuff in a garbage bag and throwing it out the window!"

If. If is a good word for me. *If* means she's still considering an action most foul.

Revalia pushes Jess's hair back from her face. "I know how you're feeling, sweetie, and trust me—forgiveness is always the key. What me and Logan have been through," she sighs. She's good at this, too! This human condition suits Revalia well! She plays her part very naturally, very smoothly. I think I may have underestimated her because I see Jess's eyes soften, and her body slumps forward toward Revalia in a receptive way. "I know it doesn't compare, but I understand the frustrations of being in a relationship. When you guys cool down, you need to talk this out with him. When you're not raging so hard and can analyze the situation with a clear mind, then reach out to him. But for now, don't be so quick to snap. You might do something you'll regret later."

"Thank you," Jess smiles.

I mean, she actually *smiles*! The man she devoted her whole adult life to just got caught with another woman, and Revalia is able to make her *smile*? It's possible the universe has turned upside down!

Revalia straightens up and walks to the door with a new air of confidence as if she's won some grand prize trophy. "Well, then," she says, "I think Tara is gonna want to start heading back in a little bit, so we'll be waiting for you guys."

"You can't understand, can you?" Jess asks after Revalia leaves.

"What do you mean?"

"What it's like. Ya know, to love someone so hard. To put everything of yourself on the line for them, only to be crushed and defeated." She starts to tear up again.

Her words touch me deeply. No, I don't know. But I do know. I know there's a hollow pit in my soul. I know I have a feeling I've lost something or someone somewhere along the way in my clandestine journey. And I know that empty feeling is somehow connected to the path I'm on right here, right now. The path I fear will lead to the Nowhere...

"It's complicated for me," I answer.

A heavy sensation warms in my chest, and I look down and clutch my medallion. The energy throbs inside of it, radiating against the palm of my hand. Where Revalia succeeded in her humanness with Jess, I will overcome with a little touch of darkness. I relax my muscles and tap into my *de-gelic* nature, and in my hand, I draw out a little sliver of darkness—a tiny bit of demonic energy, like blackened dust particles the human eye cannot observe. I walk to Jess, and in an act resembling Revalia's "human comfort," I sweep more strands of hair away from Jess's bloodshot eyes. But in this gesture, I am able to sprinkle her with the essence of the pendant, pushing the misty darkness deep into her mind.

"It'll be okay," I say. "But ya know what they say—once a cheater, always a cheater."

Jess's eyes go dark as I watch her body absorb my power. Something has awakened inside her, like a dark switch flicking on the dormant blackness in her soul. She stares straight ahead in a trance-like state, in deep contemplation, letting the energy of the shadows fill her mind and travel throughout her body. I snap my fingers in front of her face, startling her back to reality. "We should go," she says in a daze.

"Yes. Yes, we should."

CHAPTER SEVENTEEN

ALWAYS FOR YOU

Steve met us with the van and a restocked cache of supplies at the head of the North Kaibab Trail. The next leg of our "Wild West Tour" was supposed to be the scenic drive to Grand Canyon West and an afternoon exploring the Hualapai Indian Reservation and touring the Grand Canyon Skywalk Bridge. The prospect of the Skywalk Bridge had enticed me, as it's a glass-bottomed, horseshoe-shaped bridge that extends over the West Rim. There's nothing but panes of glass separating you from the deep expanse of two-thousand feet to the bottom of the canyon. I imagined walking the Skywalk Bridge would feel a lot like floating, or at least give the sensation of it. Maybe it would have made me feel like my old self again, floating in Ilarium, because, lately, I've kind of lost sight of who I am.

Who am I?

What have I become?

What the hell am I doing here?

There are many different versions of me—the dutiful daughter, the steadfast best friend, the insolent child, the independent free-spirit, the angel, the human, the demon. The overwhelming onslaught of emotions and memories has clouded me, jaded me, made me *change*.

I slowly give into the darkness, because each moment that passes, I become less and less conscious of this medallion I wear. It protects me by creating the illusion of an actual person, it gives me power to control and manipulate situations at my will, and it also comforts me and acts as some dark sedative.

And I know this is wrong—all of it!—everything I have done to this point could have probably been handled differently. I know that! But something happened to me when I fell through time and space. Something fundamentally changed inside of me, and for the first time in my existence, I wanted to do something on my own and *for myself*. *Not* in servitude to my Father. *Not* in accordance with the holy host of angels. *Not* because I was bred to believe I needed to attain some higher form of myself.

So, now we're camping out in a secluded area along the Trailhead, our "tour" being set back by yet another interruption. It seems Janice and Dylan no longer want to be a part of our tour. She's weary and frustrated and hadn't "anticipated the strenuous effort" it would take to go on such an adventure, and it wasn't what she had envisioned as her "perfect honeymoon." Right now, Janice wants to go to Vegas where she can gamble and go to shows and get pampered in spas and go clubbing at night. The outdoors stuff has "worn her down."

Steve and Tara were greatly disappointed because they take their tours very seriously—it's their livelihood! And their only goal is to make all their guests happy. Steve made some calls to his friends in the area, and someone was able to swing by and pick them up. I overheard Tara say there would be a hefty price to make these radical changes so late in the game, but Dylan had responded "no price is too high to make my bride happy." And that was that. Janice and Dylan, the sweet newlyweds with a dark secret, rode off into the night headed for the bright lights of none other than Sin City.

I don't buy Janice's story for a second because I know this turn of events has everything to do with her indiscretion with Scott. She wanted to get as far away from him—and Jess—as she possibly could, and that's understandable. If I were caught red-handed in such a compromising position, I might want to run away too.

Or kill everyone around me...

I shake my head quickly, trying to erase the thought from my mind. When I close my eyes, I see visions of the strange angel hovering in the sky. She's haunted my night dreams and has infiltrated my daydreams,

as well. Every scene I envision with her is darker and more twisted than the one before it, and I am drawn to her unapologetic demeanor—her straightforward gestures of how she doles out punishment in her cold, executioner style. In my visualizations, I stand at a distance from her and bask in the gruesomeness of her presence. But sometimes, I feel compelled to zone in on her face to watch her expressions, to glean her emotions at what she is doing, and sometimes... sometimes she looks as if she takes pleasure in the torture of the humans.

I take pleasure in the torture of the humans.

Because, as Malek confirmed, the strange angel is, in fact, me. And my dreams, whether they are during the night or during the day, aren't really dreams so much as they are memories.

Memories.

As in... things I've done, lives I've taken, fear I've instilled. Me. All me. These events reveal themselves to me, but I have no recollection of ever taking part in any of them. I'm still confused as to why I snapped into such a wild rage and went on an epic killing spree. I couldn't have systematically—and delightfully—killed people? Could I?

The zipper on my tent pulls down, and I sit up in my sleeping bag. "I'm going to do it, ya know. I made up my mind, and no one is going to stop me." Jess storms into my tent with her bold declaration, tearing me away from my enigmatic memories. "Probably when we're on the Skywalk Bridge, or close to it. Accidents happen all the time out here, ya know? I figure it'll be my last chance to be done with it all." She taps her foot on the floor and rubs her hands together, waiting for me to respond—to say something, anything. Perhaps she's looking for approval or validation.

I look around us to see if anyone else is nearby. Malek is off doing God-knows-what, and the others in the group seem to be a good enough distance away to not hear our conversation. "Why are you telling me this?" I ask.

She sits across from me on top of Malek's sleeping bag and crosses her legs. "I felt like I had to. Like, I get the sense you understand how I feel." She lowers her voice, "Like, you've done dreadful things too. I know you're not gonna tell anyone either."

I open my mouth to respond, but she cuts me off. "And listen," she says quickly, "I know there's something 'off' between you and your brother. In fact, I don't believe for a second he is your brother."

I chuckle a little at the thought. *If you only knew, dear girl.* "Oh, trust me, he is!"

"Well, it's weird. Ya know? The way he looks at you."

"What are you talking about? What do you mean by that?"

"You know the day you went out on the Rim Trail with Scott and I stayed behind with your brother? I tried to flirt with him. Had a big ole plan, too. I even made a bet with that Janice chic before she went on her excursion. I bet her ten bucks I would be able to get him to flirt back with me and maybe even *insinuate* something. Wink wink, nudge nudge. But guess what? Nothing. Nada. Zip. Zilch!"

A slight surge of jealousy jolts the pit of my stomach, but I ignore it. "So, you were mad at Scott for going on a hike with me, and you wanted to get attention from my brother?" I ask, confirming her story.

She huffs. "You mean your 'brother.'" She uses two fingers on each of her hands to make air quotes when she says the word *brother*. "Because when he's with you, he lights up something spectacular. That's not the way a brother acts around his sister. But whatever, that's your business and none of my concern." She drifts off, and I think I understand what she's saying—she longs for someone to look at her that way. She wants to be revered and adored and held to the highest of highs. Now, whether Malek feels that way about me is yet to be seen, but *she* sees something there, and she likes it, she wants it, she covets that feeling. And we all know once you start coveting your neighbors' possessions, well, that can most definitely lead to the breakage of some of those other human commandments.

We hear voices approaching and Jess shoots up from the ground. "Anyway, I'm letting you know what I've decided, and nothing you say is going to stop me."

But it's obvious she's unsure. Twitching. Nervous. She's hoping I'll talk her out of it. Tell her it's crazy talk, they'll work things out, don't be so foolish, you're being crazy, how could you ever think of doing such a thing, you're hormonal and need to ride it out, kick him out when you get home, and on and on and on with the typical human responses. People don't normally declare they plan on murdering their lovers. People don't boldly waltz into the tents of strangers and declare they are going to commit the most heinous and primal act of slaying another human being. It *is* crazy talk! She wants me to talk her out of it. Practically begging me. But I won't because it was I who stirred those feelings up inside her in the first place. I was the one who kind

of "green-lit" her plan and made her somehow feel it was okay. This display right now, her approach to me—this is the last-ditch effort of her human condition that desperately seeks salvation. Once she goes down that path, down the road of slaughter, she will never return. She will have given over to the darkness and, most likely, won't be able to come back from it.

"Why would I try to stop you?" I say.

"Okay, then," she says and backs out of my tent.

I take a deep breath, replaying Jess's plan in my mind. I had thought her words would have filled the aching void in my soul with the knowledge I would be one step closer to my destination. But they didn't. Her words don't fill in my empty gaps, it makes them bigger.

Malek comes back into the tent with a plate of food for me. "Here," he says, placing it in front of me, "I thought you would..."

I push it away. "No, thank you."

He senses my frustration. How could he not? It must be written all over my face. "What's up? What happened?"

"The girl. *My* girl. She's planning on doing it."

Malek's eyebrows raise. "Yeah?" A hopeful smile slowly creeps on his face.

I sigh. "That's the word on the street."

"Okay, okay," he says nodding his head. "This is a good step."

"What happens next?"

"Well, 'planning' and 'doing' are two different things. 'Planning' is step one. 'Doing' brings everything to fruition."

I sigh again. Sometimes speaking to Malek and deciphering his riddles are exhausting. "Okay, let's say it gets to that point... to *fruition*, as you call it."

"Then you'll be free."

I run my hands across my head and grip chunks of hair at the roots. "Can you please be straight with me right now?" I practically beg. "What does being 'free' mean?"

He laughs at my frustration. "You won't be stuck in Asphodel, for one thing. And like I told you; you'll move up the ranks of the Demonic Order, Aestrangel."

"Will I be a demon like you?"

"Only if you want to be."

"All I want is to see Camael," I say, exasperated. "That's all I've wanted throughout this entire ordeal."

"I'm sure The Morning Star can make that happen," he says.

But I'm not fully convinced. I fear he's lying to me because, in all my angelic knowledge, a demon has never been granted an audience with one of the Powers That Be.

He reaches into his backpack next to his sleeping bag and pulls out two small vials filled with a sapphire blue liquid. I remember a similar vial from when I was a human on my first Calling. I remember Aunt Ruth handing it to me and telling me about how it was my ticket back to Ilarium. I remember standing in the park with Malek before I drank it. He comforted me, told me things would be okay, told me he owed me because *I* was *his* successful Calling. "Once the girl completes the act, you and I have one more thing to do."

"I know. But I'm guessing that won't take me back to Ilarium."

He puts a vial back in his pack and hands the other to me. "No. I'm afraid it won't. But keep this one safe. You'll know when to use it."

I remember our conversation on the day I had to return to Ilarium. Aunt Ruth had given me the purple vial and told me to go back to the park where I had descended. I thought I would be alone, but Malek was there to see me off. *"You won't fail. I'll see to it,"* he had said.

"I don't need anything, especially from you. I think I've gotten myself into enough trouble as it is."

"No cost. Consider it a favor for a friend."

"We're not friends, Malek!"

"Trust me, I owe you more than you know."

I remember his unpaid debt. I fold my arms across my chest and inhale deeply. "You owe me though. You said so yourself." My voice is heightened, frantic.

He moves next to me and puts his arm around my shoulder. "I didn't forget. I made a promise to you, and that debt will be repaid. No worries."

I let my body melt into the comfort of his embrace and lean my head close to his chest. There is no heartbeat sound. No *thump-thump-thump* rhythm of the typical human organ. No blood runs in this body, at least not the kind of blood that is equivalent to our human counterparts. There is a secret stillness in his chest. Not hollow. Not empty. It is musical, like a *whooshing* sound. Something moves inside, something hums. Like ocean waves crashing on sandy shores. Like a soul waiting patiently for its mate to return.

"When it happens," I say, my voice muffled in the crook of his arm, "when we're ready to move on, we'll be together again at the end, I guess. Just like how it was the first time around."

"Seems so," he replies, but I detect a hint of sadness in his voice.

"I was so mean to you, wasn't I," I laugh, thinking back to my last moments on Earth with him.

"You've come around a little bit since then," he jokes.

I tug on his shirt to get his attention, and when our eyes meet, I see nothing in his. Not a gray storm, or a violent tornado. Not a beach backdropped by a golden sky, or the ashen landscape of Asphodel. His eyes have gone completely black, like two round pieces of onyx set in his beautifully perfect face. My own reflection doesn't even appear in the glossy orbs. What is he thinking? Why the strange countenance that is so un-Malek-like?

"You always seem to take care of me," I say searching his eyes for any kind of sign or symbol. "Why? You are like my shadow in the day, and my ray of light in the dark. And you always give me another angle, another perspective to look at the world with. Why? And how is it you can completely frustrate me, enlighten me, and excite me all at the same time? Like, what is *this*?" I touch my medallion, then grab onto his hoping to tap into his essence, to break the code, to figure him out.

He pushes some of my hair from my face and kisses my forehead, then pulls me close to his chest again and strokes the back of my neck. "Because it's about you, Aestrangel. It's always been about you and will always be about you. Always."

CHAPTER EIGHTEEN

SALVATION

I anticipate the finale of our Wild West Tour. It will be coming to a screeching halt in a short while, and tensions among everyone are at an all-time high. Steve and Tara have been on edge practically this entire vacation—with all the waiting, and rushing, and interruptions, and change of plans—I know they feel like this tour has been a failure. I can hear it in the way they speak to each other. They were fighting before about when we should leave for the West Rim because they were being conscious of our time. After our tour is over, they must head back immediately to pick up another group to take out on the road. Perhaps it will be another group of damaged angels and reformed demons to entertain? Tara insisted on leaving at daybreak so we could all get the full effect of the scenic drive, but Steve was adamant about leaving as soon as possible. He said something about his friend (the guy who picked up Janice and Dylan to take back to Vegas) knowing some kind of back road shortcut that could save us about an hour from our four-and-a-half-hour drive. "It's still gonna be scenic," I overheard him say to her, "just not the scenic we're used to."

Tara was apprehensive at first, but she ultimately gave in to him because here we are—bobbing up and down in the van as we trek

across mostly dirt-paved roads and rocky terrain. Tara had called out to us to buckle up, and we all mostly laughed it off, but right as Steve took the van in a low-lying ditch the clicking sounds of fastening belts could be heard simultaneously.

I lean my head against the window of the van and stare out into the inky black sky. The dome of the world overhead is littered with thousands of twinkling stars. They're all watching me, waiting for me to make my next move, curious as to how the ultimate finale will play out. Looking at them makes me feel small, and the weight of my mortality pulls on my chest as I realize that. Yes! I am another cog in the machine, another spoke in the wheel. And if this situation didn't involve me, it would have involved someone else, for I am replaceable—one star in a sky of millions.

Before I turn my head to look away, I witness a white streak blaze across low on the horizon—a falling star. Well, to the human perception, at least! I know what just happened. An angel was disengaged from Ilarium and is now headed toward his or her Calling.

Revalia and Lozhure are sitting together in the row behind me. They saw the angel as the falling star, too.

"Azura?" Revalia asks him.

"I don't think so," he answers. "Maybe Leonas? Sa'rai?"

"Hmmm... I don't know." She snaps her fingers. "Oh, oh, what about Maselith? She was right on the verge when we left and..."

"Yep! I think you're right," he agrees.

They continue to talk about the angels with names I do not know. Names I don't recognize. Names that have no meaning even to my de-gelic ears. I guess I have been gone from Ilarium for much longer than I originally thought.

Jess and Scott are in the row in front of me, chatting softly, giggling every now and then. She's keeping up appearances, maintaining the status quo. But I know her secret. I know the true intentions in her heart, and a part of me wishes it would all be over with as soon as possible. I tune out their meaningless conversation as the van bumps along. Tara yells at Steve to slow down a little. He apologizes to her, and to us, but I don't notice any change in the speed he's going.

The bumping didn't disturb Malek, who is sleeping like a baby in the row directly across from me. His backpack is nestled firmly in his lap, and his head is resting on his side of the window. Eyes closed, he looks so perfect and peaceful in his slumber. Perfect and peaceful, the way a true devil should. The unsuspecting human eye would never in a million years be able to peg him for what he truly is. Suave. Handsome. Charming. Everything most men aspire to be and everything most women desire to be with. I try to stifle a laugh and end up snorting through my nose. If they only knew the truth. If they could only see the darkness beneath the mask. They would not have favorable things to say then, would they? Even more so if they were able to glean the two of us together in all our deformed glory! Oh, what a pair we make—Malek with his stony, cloven hooves, and me with my blood-stained wings and slightly protruding horns. What a sight we would be if we could reveal our true selves to the world!

I laugh again to myself, and this time I don't try to hide it. I've been hiding so much for too long, that I make a promise to myself—after all this is over, I promise to be more like Malek. More carefree, and yet confident in myself. I promise that I will have renewed strength with a touch of stronger moxie. My will is strong, but I often find myself second-guessing my actions. Well, no more of that! I promise I will keep my emotions and actions cool and calm, not go spinning out of control the way the van is doing right now and...

I continue to stare at Malek's face. My eyes are focused on his bone structure, and the center of his face is clear and sharp, but behind him and around him everything is a carousel blur. I hear everyone in the van screaming as we careen out of control. Malek's eyes open and meet mine in a gaze of absolute horror. In what feels like a slow-motion dance, my body rushes up at an angle, and I am jostled back and forth in my seatbelt before the van comes slamming down sideways on the ground. Glass shatters and pops in the cabin like mini explosions all around me. It takes me a few moments to realize what just happened. We must have hit something or swerved to get out of something's way, and that sent us spinning off the road and over the side of a small cliff.

Surprisingly, Malek and I don't scream like the others. In fact, we never broke eye contact during the whole descent. For me, this accident is all too familiar, all too real, as if I've been through something similar before. This is all too reminiscent of my previous memories of my so-called human life. That time long ago when I lost my parents and my wings.

Except for the back of my head hitting the window, I think I'm okay. My side of the van lies on the ground. Malek's side is suspended in the air, and he dangles in the aisle by his seatbelt. Once he's processed

what has happened, his eyes open wide with terror, and he frantically looks around. His backpack was thrown from his lap in the accident—the backpack that contains his blue liquid vial. Retrieving it seems to be a priority.

"Everyone okay?" Lozhure calls out.

Malek fusses with his belt, trying to get it off. "You good?" he asks me. I nod and pat my shorts pocket, letting him know my vial is still on me. He nods back and replies, "We're good!" answering for us both.

Jess is wailing in the seat in front of me. "Scott's not moving, and... oh, God! Where's Steve? Where's Tara and Steve?"

"It's okay. It's all okay," Lozhure says, trying so hard to calm Jess down. "Can you reach him?"

"Yes!" she calls back.

"Is he breathing?" he shouts.

"Yes! Yes! Please, please hurry! Please! He needs help!"

Lozhure unbuckles Revalia and helps her to stand. "Come on, baby," he says softly, as he guides her over the van seats. "I'm going to push out the back door," he announces. "The front window is gone."

And so are Steve and Tara, I think. *Probably thrown from the van.*

Revalia gets out of the van, and I hear Lozhure tell her to get as far away as she can. At the exact same time, I start to smell burnt rubber coming from the front of the van, and puffs of smoke begin to make their way into the cabin.

"Oh, God! Oh, God! Don't leave me!" Jess cries, and I'm not sure exactly to whom it is she's talking. Is she talking to Lozhure, begging him not to leave her in the burning van, or is she crying to Scott, begging him not to die—not to leave her in this mortal shell?

Malek hops over the seats, frantically looking for the pack. "Come on," he calls to me. "You gotta get yourself out of here."

"I'm okay. I'm okay," I say dismissively. "I need a second or two."

That's not entirely a lie. My head hurts from the fall, and when I look down at my lap, my leg is cut open from my knee to my upper thigh—a piece of glass juts out from the bloody wound, and I can't help but wince when my brain acknowledges the laceration and processes the sensation of pain. My first step is to unbuckle myself, then quickly, but gently, hobble my way to the back of the van.

Only, I can't get the seatbelt to click open. I press the red button several times in frantic succession to no avail. My heart starts to race as the smell of the burning van gets stronger. I try to steady my breathing, so as to not have a full-blown panic attack!

"Jess?" I call to her. "Jess, you need to unbuckle you and Scott. Logan is coming back to get you."

She doesn't answer me, but I can hear her sobbing.

"Jess! Did you hear me?"

I hear the click of her belt. "Scott didn't have his belt on," she mumbles.

"Okay. Are you hurt?"

She mumbles something else unintelligible, and Malek creeps behind my seat. "Hey," he whispers in alarm, "the pack's not here. I think it got tossed out. I'm gonna go search around the accident site to see if I can find it."

I nod my head quickly.

He pauses. "You sure you're okay?"

"Yeah, yeah. Glass in the leg and head throb. Stupid belt is giving me problems..."

"Here, I'll..." He motions to come around to me, but I wave him off.

"Go. Just go. You must get the bag."

He looks at me one last time and leaves. I hear Lozhure huff, and he passes Malek on the way out. "Figures, demon!" he scolds. Malek doesn't respond, and I go back to fumbling with the seatbelt.

"Aestra? Is that Logan?" Jess cries.

Lozhure passes by my seat, and I nod at him, letting him know he needs to help them first. "I'm here, Jess," he says calmly to her. "I need you to climb to the back and out of the van. Reba is out there waiting for you. I know it hurts, but I need as much space as I can to drag Scott out of this."

"Oh, oh, okay," she blubbers as she begins stumbling over the seats.

"Lozhure!" I call. "Is he alive?"

"Yes," he answers.

I sigh in relief, and I realize that I never wanted anyone to get hurt or die in the first place. Who was I for thinking that would be a means to an end? Who was I for thinking that could be a means to *my* end?

Lozhure lifts his head, and I hear moaning from the seat. "He's starting to come out of it too. How are you doing over there?"

I tug at the belt's latch again. It still won't budge. "Fine. Just trying to work my leg into a good position."

"Don't take that glass out!" he warns. "You don't want to bleed out."

"I know, I know. I'm working on it."

"Well, you better work faster! It's getting hot in here if you know what I mean."

I lean my head back against the seat. "I know!"

Lozhure grumbles and grunts, pulling and pushing on Scott's body, heaving his limp bag of bones painfully over the seat edges. "I'll come right back for you, okay?"

"No worries, I'm right behind you," I say as the smoke gets thicker.

I lied. I'm not right behind him. There's no way I'm getting out of this as Aestra Forcas. I run my hand over my pocket and finger the blue liquid vial within. That will be my only salvation, my only chance of making it out of this.

I close my eyes as Lozhure and Scott pass over me. I close my eyes because what else am I to do? The way Jess cried for Scott in what she thought were his last moments was a proof-positive sign she was never going to go through with her plan. Her human emotions gave her the idea, and the plan, and even the mind frame to think it all up, but at the end of the day, she didn't have it in her. She couldn't have. How could she have brought on his death, when in the midst of an accident she completely lost her mind at the thought of losing Scott?

I have failed.

Again.

My leg starts to throb in rhythm with my head. I touch the back of it only to feel the sticky blood matting my hair. Despite any urgency I may feel to get myself up and out of this van that is now filled with smoke, I can't bring myself to do it. Something in the wreck of an engine sparks and pops, and I open my eyes to see the flames begin to shoot out from the front of the vehicle. I think back to when I walked with Malek and spoke with the people in our simulation. The woman in that burning car screamed and pleaded for help. I now understand how she felt as the heat and smoke overtakes me. How fitting it is I am in her exact situation—a fiery end with help a few feet away. *I'm sorry I didn't help you.*

I take the vial out of my pocket with one hand, and with the other, I clutch at my medallion.

There are more screams from the people outside. I hear Revalia's hysterical voice yelling, "Aestra? Where's Aestra? Malek! You need to get her! You bastard! Get in there and save her!"

"She was right behind me!" Lozhure screams back as something else in the van fires off with red and yellow hot tongues.

"Aestra!" Malek's wild voice gets closer. "Listen to me, Aestrangel!" he calls. "Now is the time! You must do it! Don't wait any longer!"

I open my mouth to answer him, to let him know I heard him, and that I understand, but all that comes out are labored coughs as I ingest a lung's-worth of smoke.

He's talking about the blue vial. He wants me to drink it so whatever dark spell I am under will be reversed, like it was long ago when I went back home to Ilarium from my first Calling.

"What are you talking about?" Revalia screams at him, and I hear her fists pounding on Malek's chest.

"She knows what to do..." he says, but the rest of his words are drowned out by the roaring sounds of the fire consuming the van.

I untwist the cap of the vial and stare deeply into the blue liquid. It's metallic looking, like cerulean mercury. Drinking this would save me—save whatever mortal connection I have to this world and transport me to some other dimension. Not Ilarium, I'm sure of that. Back to Asphodel? Maybe to the darkest depths of the Underworld? Maybe to the throne room of Lucifer himself?

The blue liquid is mesmerizing as I move it in little circles in front of my face. I'm hot. Dizzy. I try to hold my breath but can't help but cough.

"This isn't how it was supposed to be, Aestra!" Revalia's cry carries over the torrent of flames and exploding glass.

No, Revalia. You're right. This isn't how any of this was supposed to be.

The gods have abandoned me.

The angels have abandoned me.

Even the devils who walk amongst men have abandoned me.

I take the vial, hold it out in front of me, and empty its contents onto my sideways lap.

There is no longer any option with an easy way out. I have made this mess myself, and I know this is the right thing to do.

I can't help but smile as the heat of the burning van engulfs me, and I succumb to the gray smoke.

Death shall be my salvation.

Death shall be my sacrifice.

CHAPTER NINETEEN

THE HALL OF MIRRORS

My eyes flutter open, and as I start to come to, I gasp a waking breath into consciousness, like being reborn. The last thing I remember was red—red heat, red flames, red pain. I was numb at the end, going in and out of consciousness as I tried so hard to zone out and focus my mind on something good and positive. But there was only red as I died.

I died.

I know I died. I felt my flesh bubble up from the intense heat and ooze away. I even removed the shard of glass in my leg to allow the blood to flow out faster. Death had crept up from the soles of my feet and enveloped my entire body before gripping my throat and squeezing me to everlasting sleep. It hurt, yet there was something so peaceful and serene about it.

As I process my surroundings, I realize I am lying on the floor of a room that glitters in rows of mirrors. I extend my arms out, and while I bear the semblance of the human form, I am no longer trapped in the confines of the shape. I can look right through my arm in a colorful, semi-transparent glean. A heavy weight tugs at my back, and when I sit up, feathers tickle the back of my ethereal neck.

My wings!

I crack them out at my sides and admire the pristine white plumes. As a smile creeps upon my face, the feathers change colors—white to yellow to orange to pink—as a rush of different emotions overtakes me.

There is no pain, and I am no longer burdened with the weight of humanity or any form of a demonic presence. I am home. In Ilarium. Yet, I know I haven't regained my complete angel status because I am here in the Hall of Mirrors, and that can only mean one thing...

I will be judged.

The three judges—Och, Oethra, and Razelle—are the Cherubim, and they perform one of the most important duties for the Creator. As one of the highest levels in the Angelic Order, they judge the souls that have passed on in life to see if they will be absorbed back into the breath of the Lord, or if they are worthy enough to gain status as an Ishim.

Ishim are angelic creatures but are not technically angels. They are given wings, and a certain range of power to see the physical world, to look over their progeny, and to experience the advancements of the human condition, but they do not have the full extent of knowledge and grace as angels do.

I think Camael beat that mantra into my head so often, I can practically quote him verbatim. Bottom line is Ishim status is paradise for the human soul—the reward for a job well done in life. Well, I kinda died while in a human form. But not. What I was, what happened to me—those were all very unhuman-like and un-angel-like occurrences, and I'm not so sure the basic rules of death and judgment apply to me anymore.

I stand and spin around, in awe of my restored wings. As I twist and turn my body, I look down and see I am not grounded to a floor. My body no longer abides by any gravitational pull. I am weightless, suspended, floating above what appears to be a marble surface. I twirl in front of the giant mirrors, and my wings flash a rainbow spectrum that bounces against each image in what looks like infinity. This is everything I had hoped for. Everything I had wished for. And now I am here. Really here! I am dizzy from the images of me spinning haphazardly in the reflections, but I don't care. I would be dizzy forever if it meant I could be here always!

The mirrors suddenly go black, and I can no longer see myself and my colorful wings. "Aestra!" a harmonious voice calls out from beyond the mirrors of the hall. I freeze, anticipating what is to come. The voice

is one, but many. Stern, but melodic. And it speaks to me in the angelic language of our essences—a language I can hear only in the deepest parts of my being.

I stare at the blacked-out mirror in front of me, searching in the dark depths for a sign or an inkling of their presence. "Yes," I answer, but my voice is small, diminutive. I don't think I'm prepared for this. I wish I had more time to enjoy my return to Ilarium.

Three silver lights flicker behind the blackness of the glass. "You are here to be judged," they say at once, their singular voice like a lullaby.

I swallow hard. "Judged?"

"Yes, Aestra. Like all souls who have come through these halls, you are subjected to the same standards as all the Lord's creations."

"Because I died?"

"Because of many things. Death is just one of them."

I swallow again as the realization creeps up on me. This could very well be my last moments as a being of any kind. If they judge me and deem me unworthy, I could be reabsorbed into the breath of the Creator and cease to exist. This type of mortality had never occurred to me. My wings go blue with fear.

"You are not being considered for Ishim," they say. "Because your original design is that of angel, your judgment will lead to your permanent status as such."

"And if not?"

"You know the answer to that, Aestra," they say, confirming my suspicions.

The silver lights combine into one and push forward from the glass. The light materializes into a tall, wraithlike shape next to me. It is dressed in a hooded cloak, and its ghostly body gives off a silver translucent light. It has a face, but there is a scarred mound in the area where its eyes should be. Och takes my hand in his, and in a circular motion, waves them in the air. The mirrors spring back to life, reflecting a pink glow that lights the entire hall.

"You were angel. And you were good," he says, his voice now a singular entity. "The Lord created you from His divine breath and the oldest star-matter from the cosmos. He called you *Aestra*. His Star. The only of her kind. The child with so much hope and promise. The one to shine bright in His realm like a never-ending space of mortal diamonds."

He waves our hands again, and in the mirrors, I see multiple images of me. Images of my life—my creation, my upbringing, my training, my early life, I always was, but never was. I was formed and created, yet always existed since the dawn of time. There is no separation, no starting point of my life, yet I see the Creator's breath swirl in the open expanse of the galaxy to design my form, my shape. I see images of me singing songs in praise to the Lord. I see pinks and purples of my essence shining brighter than any other angel's in Ilarium. I see the love the Creator had for me, and I for Him.

Och continues. "As angel, you were incredibly special to many. Your mentor and guide, Camael, your sister and best friend, Revalia, all those who knew you and loved you, loved you dearly and deeply. And you loved them back."

He lets go of my hand and uses his own to wave in front of the mirrors again. This time, they glow red and fiery. "But you had a passion for something else. Something that other angels of your stature had no real connection with."

"Humans," I say.

"Humans," he repeats. "You marveled at them, were in awe of them, wished to be in their presence like no other."

"Because He made them. They are His divine creation."

"But your deep affection went further than love. You cherished their words, their music, their poetry. You were enamored by their shape and essence."

I see in the red flames indescribable images. They are more like visual emotions of joy, hope, and desire. The reflections seep out through the mirror and encircle me in a red haze, and I am filled with the memories of my earlier days. The haze tickles against my cheeks like the hands of a father caressing the face of his child. They are warming, and comforting, like home. Och snaps his misty fingers, and the red haze sucks back into the mirror.

"Was it wrong to feel that way?" I ask. "Should I not have cared so much for them?"

He shakes his head. "No. It's what pleased the Lord so much. You were able to have a love for them like no other angel before or after you. You were the only one to understand them, and it was so much like the way He felt about them when He designed them. It's what made Elohim love you even more."

Elohim. Och refers to the Father as Elohim. This term is not used often, as it translates directly to the word *father*. And I understand Och

means to equate the Creator as my true father—not the heavenly creator of all, but a father in the sense of a parent.

"As angel, Aestra, you are deemed worthy of Ilarium."

Silver light once again seeps out from the mirror and incorporates itself with Och. Och's figure shifts to the stately figure of a goddess with long, silver hair draped over one shoulder. The eyeless face also transforms, and two pale blue eyes emerge from what was Och's scars. However, in place of a mouth, there are silver hooks looping through what looks like protruding skin. This is Oethra, the judge of the earthly domain, and while she has no mouth to project her angelic voice, I can hear her through her piercing eyes—her voice like tiny bells in my mind.

<As human, you found the world to be strange. Not the human world— the angelic world. The human world was strange in a good way. It was new. It was exciting. And you were so determined to please the Lord. You were more than comfortable in your earthly skin, walking on your human feet, adjusting to the nuances of human life.>

I look to the mirror and images of my first time on Earth appear. Aunt Ruth in the park, the brownstone in Brooklyn, the school with scores of human teenagers. Music, laughter, tears, books. The memories flood me, and I can't help but fondly smile. It's as if I'm watching a recording of my time there.

<Your intentions were good, as you strived to successfully complete your Calling in any way that you saw possible. You started out on the right path, but perhaps your connection to humanity was a little bit too strong. Perhaps it was a mistake to send you on an earthly Calling in the first place because your kinship with mankind left you open and susceptible to certain temptations.>

Some of the mirrors go black during specific scenes as if they are being censored from my view. "Hey, wait!" I protest. "Why are some images darkened? Why are there things I cannot see?"

<Everything about your Calling has been erased,> she explains. <You are still bound by the oath you formed with The Morning Star, and those details will be hidden from you forever.>

I clench my fists as anger starts to rise within me. Oethra gives me a sharp look, and I calm myself down.

<You were human,> she says, <and while you did questionable things, you did them as a human with good intentions. Your nobility was severely misguided, as you embraced humanity with more than open arms.>

My cheeks go hot in embarrassment, yet I'm not sure why.

<As human, Aestra, you are deemed worthy of Ilarium.>

A third silver light streams from the mirrors and binds itself to the figure of Oethra. The spectral shape shrinks considerably in size and takes on the guise of a young girl, as the room goes completely dark. The only light in the hall is the silver glow of Razelle, the Keeper of Secrets, forever in fledgling form to preserve innocence and new beginnings. Her face is complete with sparkling green eyes, but she is more translucent than Och and Oethra. When Razelle makes even the most subtle of movements, she seems to disappear like a fog monster in the misty morning.

"After your Calling on Earth," she begins, "you suffered great loss. You suffered much pain and agony that your angelic mind and human mind could not reconcile. And in that moment of doubt and anger, you became estranged—estranged from your Father, estranged from Ilarium, and estranged from yourself. Your rational thinking was hindered by a sense of vengeance and self-preservation, and quite arguably, a sense of desperation." Razelle extends her small arm and points to one of the mirrors. It flickers on and a scene unfolds. A scene that seems all too familiar. A scene that I can hardly bear to watch. The room goes cold, and I squint my eyes, but Razelle scolds me. "Watch!" she commands. "For only as an outsider will you understand."

The strange angel from my visions sprints across a stormy sky. She races in circles like a black blur and shapes the clouds into large funnels at her will. Rain and hail pummel the ground below her. Lightning crashes down in furious blasts of destruction. Thunder rattles rooftops of the houses in the town. The people in the homes lift their heads to the sky and beg for mercy from the strange creature. "Oh, great Aestrangel! Oh, Dark One! We beseech thee!" they lament. A prayer rises into the atmosphere, a prayer that they have memorized and chant together at their final hour: *Oh, Great One, we bow—in your presence, at your mercy. For you, and you alone, can light the blackened sky.* The angel holds the monstrous funnel clouds in place as she appears to contemplate the song of the people. But with one flick of her wrist, she unleashes hell upon them and sets the twisters loose to decimate the people who sought her mercy.

I did that.

That was me.

"You were commissioned to obliterate the bloodline of your Calling," Razelle says as she wipes the images off the mirror. "You accepted the mission from The Morning Star in return for the erasure of your

memories. When you succeeded in this task, you were flung through time and space—hurtled through the chasm of what is known and not known for lifetimes, centuries, eons, but mere minutes."

I hang my head low as the information sinks into me.

"Even though you were estranged, Aestra, these acts are acts that cannot be forgotten. As Aestrangel, you are *not* deemed worthy of Ilarium."

I feel sick in my stomach. I feel sick and alone. I try to process the horrors I have wrought, but it still feels like that was someone else, some*thing* else. I still can't understand what could have happened to have made me go completely ballistic like that.

Razelle transforms into a ball of light and launches herself into a mirror. The room lights up with sparkling lights illuminating a golden chandelier overhead. Every mirror twinkles and sings, and a warm feeling permeates the room. Och, Oethra, and Razelle have once again incorporated as one being, one Cherub, one judge, and their collective voice reverberates in the hall.

"Your second time on Earth was a confusing one for you," they begin. "You had a Calling for The Morning Star, but you never fully committed to the cause. You struggled. You questioned, much like in the vein of how you had once questioned the Lord. Yes, you were blinded by your newfound powers and deceptive mission, but in the end, in your angel heart, your astral gene, you *knew*. And with that knowledge, you were able to make a choice, a sacrifice. You sacrificed your unholy self to the Powers That Be in the ultimate act of sorrow and surrender. To the Creator. To the Lord. To your Father. To *God*. And because of that, Aestra, you have been forgiven. You have proven to Him that you are truly sorry for the actions you have committed, and He deems you worthy of Ilarium."

I pause, a little confused. "Wait? What does this mean then?"

Their voice gets louder, more melodic. "He's chosen you, Aestra."

"Why? Chosen me for what?"

"For eternity," they say, and the brightness in the hall dims to a candlelight. They are gone, leaving me alone with their cryptic answer.

I bite my lower lip and wring my hands together with anticipation. What does all this mean? What happens to me now? The Cherubim were not helpful or clear about the next steps!

Suddenly, one of the mirrors folds open like a door on a hinge. On the other side of it stands Revalia. Her bruise-colored wings are spread wide open, and she smiles brightly at me. She is exactly how I remembered in her angelic form—not the meddling human who did nothing for my earthly cause. My feelings toward her are jumbled right now. I don't know whether I want to embrace her or turn from her in contempt.

My mind is made up when she calls to me. "Aestra!" she gushes with her tender voice. She sounds like a choir of angels singing in a celestial amphitheater. I know that voice. I remember that voice. I can't help but smile as my good memories and thoughts of her come rushing back.

She embraces me. I bury my head in the crook of her neck, and inhale her pink essence, filling up on her compassionate love. Our wings lock around each other sending electric waves throughout our essences. We stand there, smothered in an angel's kiss, hinged to each other in a lingering hold.

"I'm sorry, Lia," I whisper.

She strokes my hair down my mid-back. "It's okay," she coaxes. "All is forgiven. I'm so glad you've come home."

I want to say, "Me too," but the words never make it out of my mouth or my mind. She discontinues our embrace and holds me at arm's length, staring at me, taking in the full majesty of my returned angel form. "You're even more glorious than I remembered," she sighs, and my feathers rapidly flash a myriad of colors.

"I feel different," I say. "Off." Because I do. I'm a little off-balance and shaky. I know I am home, but I can't put my finger on it—something doesn't *feel* right.

She waves her hand in front of her face as if to brush away my concerns. "Yes. I know. Sometimes coming back makes you feel a little unsettled. I get this tight feeling," she brings her hands to her throat, "right around here."

"Yeah, like a big lump!"

She giggles. "Feel like you're gonna throw up or cry?"

My feathers flash pink, and I give a little sigh, "Yeah, something like that."

"I wouldn't worry too much about it. I get that weird feeling every time I come back. You'll shake it off in no time." She tucks in her wings and reaches for my hand. "Come," she says. "We need to go somewhere." She weaves her fingers through mine and squeezes my hand.

I cock my head to the side. "Where are you taking me?"

"We need to go to The Observatory. He's waiting for you."

I can only dream of who she's referring to, because everything I've done so far, everything I've experienced, has kind of led up to this very moment. "He?" I ask, waiting for confirmation.

"Yes, silly!" she smiles. "*He*. Camael eagerly awaits your return!"

I sigh when she says his name. "Camael," I repeat under my breath. "Then what are we waiting for? Let's go."

CHAPTER TWENTY

RECKONING

We venture into the Temple and pass the awe-stricken eyes of a plethora of angels. They stare me down, some turn up their noses, some wince in disgust, and others have their mouths open wide in shock. There are a few who look upon me with love and forgiveness, but they are few and far between. Their looks make me uncomfortable and uneasy—like I'm an outsider, like I have unholy feet and am stepping on sacred ground.

Revalia leads me to the golden door of The Observatory. "Never mind their curious eyes, Aestra." She touches the bronze carving of a scepter, and the door begins to creak open. "Having you back in Ilarium makes some of them nervous. Some of them look at you like..."

"An infection?" I interrupt.

She rubs the side of her head. "Well, I wouldn't go *that* far, but well, for lack of a better term."

"Tainted," I offer as a more appropriate descriptor.

She snaps her fingers. "Yes! Tainted is more like it. They feel you've been tainted with humanity."

The door finally stops creaking and is fully opened. "That's kinda funny," I say, "because that's what they had said about you, isn't it?"

She doesn't respond, and I presume my words cut her deep. I give her one last look before entering The Observatory and notice a subtle sadness in her blue eyes. Perhaps she's pondering her role in the Angelic Order. Perhaps she's opening her own eyes to an independent thought.

"Wish me luck," I say and walk through the threshold.

She gives me a soft smile and a wave before closing the door behind me.

The room itself throbs with its own life force. The energy source in the center of the room lights the entire chamber with an electric golden glow. I remember not to get too close to the pit because it is said the source can hypnotize even the Lord Himself. A figure moves in the corner of the room, and I cry out, "Camael!"

Appearing from the shadows outside of the source's light, Camael floats toward me in all his splendid glory. He's chosen to greet me in his human shape, but like I've always said, I don't know why he bothers. His strong Dominion powers shine brightly through any form he wishes to appear in, and his true self always penetrates through his chosen guise. When he smiles, a ray of white light washes over my face and covers me with a warming sensation of love, and I bask in the moment.

"Aestra," he sighs, and I run to him and toss my body into his outstretched arms. Simultaneously, we wrap our wings around each other and remain in our embrace for what seems like hours. "I've missed you." His voice echoes in my mind. His soft words tickle my senses, yet I sense there's an underlying sorrow in his demeanor—the way he prolongs our hold, the way his feathers delicately caress the tips of mine, the way he dims his light that encircles us.

"I have missed you too," I say, pulling away from him and observing him at close range.

He struggles to smile. "But you are here now, and we can all rejoice in that. You're home, Aestra, my star. You're home, and I couldn't be happier."

I have so many questions for him, and so many times I had planned out exactly what I was going to say, but as I stand here in front of him, in his holy presence, the words escape me as I submit to the feelings of love and joy. After a few moments of utter happiness, I finally ask him, "What happens next? What is to become of me?"

"Don't worry about that now. Let's just enjoy your return and…"

"Please, Camael. I've come so long and so far to be here with you. I need something to look forward to, something to give me a grounded, concrete hope."

He floats a few inches away from me. My words must make him uneasy. I know he's thinking my response to him was the exact response of a human, for only a human has desire for the context of hope, of a future, of something to keep them going along in their pathetic little lives. I am still tainted and might always be so. There's still a splinter of humanity stuck deep inside my astral essence, and it may never be eradicated, no matter how hard the Powers That Be try to change it.

"Well," he begins, "there is one thing I am certain of—there will be no more Callings for you. You will be assigned another role which has not yet been determined, but it must be something special as the Lord has chosen you from the beginning of time. Now that you are back, we can all begin anew—a fresh start. We can make things right again."

He floats over to the right side of the room, where hanging on the rocky wall is the World Window draped in a red velvet cloth. He removes the cloth and reveals the mirror. I remember this mirror from long ago when Revalia and Lozhure dragged me here to steal a glance at my Calling. The Window is the tool that allows angels to view the human world. Whatever an angel wishes to see, the Window will reveal it. If an angel is matched to a Calling, the Window will show that, too. I know that all too well.

"As one of the Lord's brightest stars, you can have much influence over the human race," he says, folding the velvet material and placing it on a wooden chest beside the mirror. "There is still a lot of good you can accomplish for the Creator."

Back to servitude? I can't help but think to myself.

Suddenly, I fear Camael has read my thoughts, and I clamp my hand quickly over my mouth, embarrassed, as if I had spoken those words out loud. He looks at me oddly—cocks his head to the side and slightly narrows his eyes as if to say, "What did you do that for?" I lower my hand and dumbly shrug my shoulders.

Camael can read everyone's thoughts. Why didn't he hear mine?

Camael continues speaking to me about how important it will be for me to accept whatever role the Lord has determined for me, but I zone him out and *think*.

Do you still love me like you did?

Am I still your worthy child?

Helloooo! Can you hear me over there?

I turn my head, I raise my voice even louder, screaming my thoughts in his direction.

Camael! Oh, Camael!

Do you always blindly follow what you're told?

Do you always do without thinking?

Do you ever wonder if you're a slave?

He snaps his fingers at me. "Aestra? Aestra, are you paying attention to what I'm saying?"

I rapidly blink my eyes. "Yes. Yes. Every word." I lie.

"Good. Come here, then."

I float over to meet him by the Window, but the only thing that consumes me is this: *Camael cannot read my thoughts anymore.* "Camael? I know about what I did. You don't need to show me any more than what I saw in the Hall of Mirrors. I know about my rejection of the Father, my time on Earth... and, well, it's not that I don't want to serve the Creator, but I'm having trouble understanding some things."

"What things?"

"Well, for one, I don't remember anything about my Calling. All the mirrors were blackened out and I..."

"That's not for me to tell you," he interrupts.

"Yes, I know, but..."

"Those are memories you chose to have extracted from your astral record. Any mention of him or of his name is never—*can never*—be spoken of."

Him?

My Calling was a male?

I gaze at the Window and notice its intricate design. From afar, the Window appears to be a giant tapestry of ever-changing images. I start to feel fuzzy and unbalanced. The more I stare at it, the more I feel weird and uneasy. Camael continues to talk about the Window. Something about how it has great power and all that junk. Again, I tune him out because I think I'm remembering something.

No.

I know I'm remembering something...

The night Revalia and Lozhure brought me to The Observatory.

"The Window scans you in a way," Lozhure had said. "When you approach it, its power *reads* you, and if you've been matched to your Calling that will be all you see."

"Like spying?"

Revalia huffed. "Sure. If you want to call it that. I like to think of it as watching. But it feels so good to get to know your Calling before you get there. It gives me more confidence, ya know? Like, I'll be better equipped to handle her."

"It's power," I said. "A power over your Calling."

"No. Not necessarily a 'power' in the way that you mean it," Lozhure replied.

"But isn't it? Isn't it a power that only the Dominions have? And if they wanted us to be able to watch our callings, don't you think Camael would have held the class right here in this room to give everyone a taste?" I yelled.

Revalia tried to calm me down. "Aestra, listen, I brought you here because I want you to see."

"See what?"

"Your Calling. I don't want you to be left in the dark. I want you to have the upper hand, so you know what you're dealing with. So you don't have to go through the hurt and pain like I had to."

"No. No thank you. I will meet my Calling when Camael says it's time to meet."

"Please, listen to me!" Her voice was frantic.

Suddenly, Lozhure was behind me, holding onto my arms, forcing me closer to the Window. I tried to fan out my wings in defense, but his body locked them in place. I thrashed myself from side to side, hoping to wiggle free from his grasp, but it was no use as he drove me closer and closer to the Window. I shut my eyes as tight as I could.

"Please! Please, Aestra! Be still," Revalia begged. "Just open your eyes, Aestra. Open your eyes."

"It's okay," Lozhure whispered in my ear. "Just look. It's so wonderful!"

"Please let me go," I cried.

"Aestra! Just look!" Revalia repeated.

With my eyes closed, I heard sounds coming from the Window—people-sounds, Earth sounds, winds, and rains, and conversations, and birds, and animals, and technology, and everything else.

"Oh, my word!" Revalia yelled. "Look! Look! Look! There he is! He's so beautiful!"

"I forgive you," I said to Lozhure, still not opening my eyes. "I forgive both of you."

"Oh, no, no, no! He's gone! He's gone!" Revalia exclaimed.

Lozhure relaxed his hold on me, and I opened my eyes. *Too soon.* I caught a glimpse of a set of deep brown eyes before the image faded to black.

I blink my eyes rapidly again, the present moment coming back into focus, my present surrounding taking root in my consciousness. I nod my head at Camael a few times while he speaks so he thinks I am paying attention to what he's saying. And like pieces of a jigsaw puzzle working their way to form a larger picture, fragments of images and conversations start to take shape in my memory. Nothing is in chronological order at first, but slowly, I begin to see. Slowly, I begin to understand.

"Jake?" I whisper.

"What was that you said, Aestra?" Camael asks.

"Jake. Who's Jake?" I repeat.

Camael's face twists. His lips suck into his mouth and his eyes widen, as the memories continue to open in my mind's eye.

"Jake!" I say with confidence. "Jake Parker! He was my..."

And it hits me.

And I gasp, the wind knocked out of me.

I struggle to breathe.

Struggle to stand.

Struggle to keep calm.

Because I remember.

I remember everything...

My mind remembers. My heart remembers. Every ounce of my being remembers! Jake Parker! My Calling! Like a dam coming apart at the seams, the flood of emotion overwhelms me. I loved him! Our astral genes connected in a way I had never experienced before. He was *my* star with his haunting brown eyes, sweet gentle kisses, and his human touch that opened me to pleasures I never knew possible. He was my soulmate. And I saved him! I helped him to be the man he became—the doting father, the wise teacher, a good husband, a leader, a man respected. He shaped the world with the thousands upon thousands of children's lives he touched. He inspired them. Challenged them to meet their potential. Lifted them to higher standards to improve upon the world—the Lord's most precious creation!

"Aestra, are you okay?" Camael says after a few moments.

"It was you who put me in this room, wasn't it?"

He doesn't respond. He shines his white light in my direction.

"Wasn't it?" I demand.

"You remember?" he asks.

I lower my head in a deep nod. "Everything."

His wings extend at his sides. They pulse with a deep, navy-blue color, and I know he's trying to offer me some sort of angelic explanation. "Aestra, it was the only way," he says extending his hands in surrender. "I suggested you be sent to The Observatory after your indiscretion with the boy only because the alternative the other Powers had offered was your banishment. It was for your own good. I couldn't let them expel you." His voice is sad, and a part of me almost feels sorry for him.

Almost...

"So, you left me here to rot?"

"No! Never!" he cries. "That was never the intent! I had hoped you would learn from the humans and pass that wisdom on to the other angels who were headed on their Callings. You just got..." his voice trails.

"Distracted? Preoccupied? What? Did you *not* think I was going to watch the man I loved? I studied every move of his entire life!"

Camael sighs heavily. "You squandered your time, Aestra."

I remember the words of the Lord when I came face-to-face with him: *Child, you have squandered your time spent in The Observatory,* he had said right before I looked upon his demonic face, right before he told me Jake would not be granted entrance into Ilarium as an Ishim. Rage swells inside me, rising from the pit of my stomach with an acidic feeling. Hot, poisonous anger begins to work its way into the very marrow of my astral soul, and without even thinking about it, my wings crack open at my sides and hum with a delicate gray aura. A pounding pressure works its way against my temples and to the center of my forehead. Camael is clearly taken off guard by this, as he takes a swift step sideways.

"That's exactly what he said to me. I *squandered* my time. But I observed. I watched. I witnessed. And for Jake to have been denied Ishim was a farce!" My voice roars, echoing off The Observatory walls. "Of all the wretched people who have passed through the Halls, Jake was one of the better ones! He should have been exalted in the holy light of the father for all of eternity!" With my last breath, a torrent

of violent wind rushes through the room, causing Camael to stumble backward an inch.

He rights himself and steps forward, as if to calm me down. "Aestra, I..."

"I needed you," I plead. "Jake was a good man, and he was ... gone. Lights out! Why didn't you help me then? That's when I needed you the most, Camael!" Tears of sadness and anger spring in the corners of my eyes. It stings my essence like something vile and toxic as it descends my cheek. *Angels aren't supposed to cry.*

"We all decided, Aestra. All The Powers. We felt it was in your best interest to absorb his soul into the Heavenly Breath. We gave our recommendation to the Creator, and He made His final decision."

My feathers tremble, and I take a slow, deep breath. I rotate my shoulders forward to try to calm the quivering, but that doesn't help. Fury takes hold of my body, and I'm not sure how much longer I can control the pressure of...

"You did this to Jake? You denied him Ishim? You played a part in all of this?" I ask. But I know the answer already.

He nods, regretfully. "Yes. That's why there is forgiveness needed on both sides. I would have never intentionally hurt you. You are my star. My Aestra. You are so special to me, like a daughter. You are unlike any other angel."

I've heard enough. A thin, red veil drips over my eyes, clouding my vision, as pure wrath bursts in my chest. Like a weed infecting the deep brown earth, its tentacles writhe their way through every inch of me, taking root in every aspect of my being. An electric shock jolts me from within, petrifying my once vibrant white quills and charring my feathers to a burnt black. The smell of burning flesh permeates the air, and Camael chokes from the scent. *It smells like the night I died.*

I close my eyes. "You're a failure yourself, Camael," I say sharply, but the sound of my voice is nearly unrecognizable. I speak with the voice of my inner self—a mechanical timbre of metal blades scraping against each other. "What right do you have to pass judgment on me when you couldn't even succeed in your own Calling?"

I envision Lilith and Samael tangled in a loving embrace in the cave beside the ocean while a forlorn Camael watches them from a distance in despair. With my astral hands, I take the vision, crumble it into a black ball and throw it in Camael's direction. He staggers backward as the image enters his astral mind. He gasps and tries to protest, but he is left speechless by the ancient memories.

Yes. I am unlike any other angel in the Creator's astral bloodline because not only have I been *infected* with humanity, but I have tasted darkness in its purest form. I think of Malek and his deep honey-wine kisses. He gave this to me. He gave me the strength to understand. To see. To *become*. To transcend.

Camael is upright and steady again, still trying to coax me. Still trying to calm me. But he can't. I am too far gone to be stopped. And to be honest, I don't want to be stopped.

I stretch my fingers out and will them to elongate. They extend to twice their original length, and in place of fingernails, I desire pointed, metal claws. I can't help but laugh as my shape bends to my command.

I sideswipe my long index finger, and Camael goes smashing into the wall, right underneath the Window. His astral form crashes hard against the stone, and the tapestry of the Window rattles against its fasteners. A small crack in the glass spiders up from the bottom-left corner to the center of the Window making the images of the human world appear warped and jagged. But isn't that how they really are? With their imperfections, and disgraceful intentions, and their ugliness, and their temptations. Maybe now the angels will see the people for what they really are—twisted reflections of their own astral essences.

Camael starts to scream as I approach him. I bring my hands in front of me and flick each of my metal-bladed fingers in succession. "Do you know how it feels to have everything you love taken away from you?"

With each movement of my blades and without even touching him, Camael's quills are viciously cut from his back, and I smile as his white feathers litter the cavern floor. "Aestra, I..." he begs frantically in pain and in terror. There's no fighting back for Camael. It's not in his astral gene to do harm to anyone. He will beg and plead, but he will not retaliate against me.

The room starts to rumble and shake, and the door to The Observatory opens wide bringing in a gale of wind from the Temple. The wind begins to swirl next to the energy source and a rushing vortex opens in the floor. Objects from the chamber become unhinged from their resting places and are sucked into the chasm. I lose my footing for a second but move closer to Camael so I'm out of the quagmire's pull.

"Do you know what it's like to have everyone you've ever loved and trusted turn their backs on you?" I say as I claw my hands up and down

in the air in front of me. As I do this, Camael's human shape begins to flicker in and out with his white light. What was once his face is now shredded gaps of light, like torn-up pieces of paper.

The mouth of the vortex grows, and it starts to pull me to it. It's for me, and I know what it's there for. I know it won't be long before I am sucked into the pit of Hell. But I am not yet finished.

I still see red. The red veil. The madness. The rage.

The retribution.

I kneel in front of Camael—his mangled, weakened body. I grab his shoulders and dig my claws deep into his being. "Do you know what it's like to watch the ones you love die?"

"Oh, Aestra," he sighs weakly, apologetically.

I press down harder, my hands entering his chest, and reaching into his astral heart. "Do you know what it's like to die?"

"Aestra! No! Please! Stop!" he cries as I ram my talons into the inner workings of his body. His white light violently flashes before sputtering out. In the distance, I hear angels wailing and screaming for the Lord to offer some assistance to the unseen massacre in The Observatory. While they don't know what has transpired, they can sense there is a dangerous presence looming in the shadows. One that Ilarium has not felt for an awfully long time.

He never does intervene though.

I remove my arms from Camael's distorted and lifeless angel shape.

But the vortex is waiting for me.

And I am ready.

So, I take a step back and allow myself to freefall down its throat.

CHAPTER TWENTY-ONE

THE CHOSEN

I've known pain and agony on many diverse levels, and to this, I am no stranger. I fall again, down the rabbit hole, down the spiraling abyss of nothingness and eternity. I fell once before, long ago, and I had been scared because the further I fell, the less I felt the presence of the Creator. That pain had struck me so deeply, and I almost wasn't able to continue my existence. I had allowed my rage and anger and hatred to consume me completely, and it had physically hurt to be cast out.

And now? I have destroyed holy life, snuffed out the glorious white light of my mentor and left the torn-up shards of his wasted essence on the sacred Observatory floor.

For these sins, I fall, yet I feel no remorse. I feel no guilt for what I have done. The Creator has washed his hands of me and has flushed me down his astral toilet.

And I feel no pain.

In fact, there is a calming sensation that works its way into me—even though I career wildly in a spiral motion, even though my essence is being torn apart at the seams and reassembled into grotesque puzzle pieces. What was once eyes are now deep, hollowed-out slats. What

once was a torso is now a mass of tentacles that wraps its arms around itself. I grow, I shift, and I change.

I become corporeal for a split second, and then the gravity force rips that body to shreds and I am formed into something different. Then the process starts all over again. Something is trying to define me, figure me out, and create a casing for me to compartmentalize my soul, causing me to die a continuous, repeated death, like a radio transmission stuck on a loop. Sometimes I get the feeling it is trying to kill me for good, but it can't. So, it must rethink how it will create me again. And every time, there is no pain, just strength, an increase in power, and an increase in ability.

I black out for a little bit, and when I come to, I am lying in a green field of purple flowers. I move each appendage of my body and try to figure out what has become of me—what shape did the Forces in the Abyss fashion for me to be in? But it's me, the same as I was before—Aestra with arms and fingers and legs and toes and a human body. *Human, but not,* because I tingle all over, like being massaged in pine needles.

The flowers around me have glittery, jeweled buds and sing a harmonious song. I sit up and pluck one from the ground so I can further inspect it. It screams as I rip it from the root, cutting it off from its essential power source. The petals are soft and veiny, and they are perfectly identical in shape and size, but upon closer inspection, the glittering bud in the center is not a gem, but an eye that blinks and stares at me with a pained expression. I throw the flower to the ground in disgust and look over my shoulder. Smoky air billows in gray tufts behind me. The eerie purple flowers close their eyes and bend their stems in a uniformed curtsy.

Asphodel.

I'm back in Asphodel, and I can't say that I am surprised because I had an inkling of a feeling I would end up back here in some capacity.

Something stirs in the smoke. The gray waves become distorted and jagged, and a great clashing and clanging sound echoes in the distance. Something is approaching—something heavy and large, like metal scales rubbing across the muscular back of a fairy tale dragon. But I know this isn't *something* that is making its way toward me. Rather, it's some*one*.

Malek.

Black, gnarled horns poke their way out of the gray fog, and as he lifts his head from behind the shadows, his demon visage is extinguished to the one that is so familiar to me—my brother. He approaches me, stepping on the purple flowers and crushing them into a path of broken stems and bloody eyes. I ignore their screams. I hear nothing but the rhythm of his monster breath quickening as he gets closer, and I rise to greet him.

"I was wondering when you would be back," he says with a sly grin. I can't help but smile back at him. He never fails to entrance me, and I am thankful he is here. In the past, I know I had tried extremely hard to deny him, but through it all, Malek Forcas has been my rock.

"How did you know?" I ask.

"I didn't. I had a feeling you might. I get a sense our way of things is better suited for now."

I clear my throat.

"I'll go out on a limb and say you didn't get the answers you were looking for," he says.

"Camael lied to me, Malek. He lied!" I say, and there's a bit of disbelief in my voice. "All of them turned their backs on me. They all betrayed me." To say the words out loud is like saying them in a dream. It's hard to reconcile the betrayal in my mind, considering my bond to Camael was so strong for so long. It still feels unreal.

Malek's eyes soften to a light gray color. "Because they fear you, Aestrangel. They fear your power and glory. They fear what you are capable of."

I throw my head up to the sky and breathe in. My long hair brushes against my folded wings and tumbles to the ground tickling the back of my ankles. There is no sun in Asphodel. Well, in my version of Asphodel, at least, because this is the place constructed by my own will and desires. *Whatever is in your heart, whatever you want to see, or experience is directly at your disposal,* Malek had told me the first time I'd ended up here, but at that time, my heart was shadowed with despair over Jake. I hadn't been able to look past that or feel anything other than the heaviness of that loss. "What I am capable of," I repeat under my breath and remember the time when I was able to create the vision orb in the palm of my hands. What if I had that same power and control right now?

I fan my wings out at my side and bring my arms together in front of me. *Just what am I capable of? Just what is it they fear?* I close my eyes

and think of Ilarium with its beautiful landscape and glorious splendor. The sun and moon were always within our vision and...

A warm sensation radiates against my eyelids, and a bright light brings colorful speckles sailing across my closed vision. I flutter open my eyes and see I have brought the sun to Asphodel. My Asphodel. Without further hesitation, I lock my hands together and set myself on my heels. With one knee bent, I jump and shoot like a canon toward my manufactured sun. My wings crack back at an angle, and I am soaring like a bird through the sky, headed for the orange ball.

Not *like* a bird, though. *As* a bird.

My body morphs into a glittering red and gold feather phoenix racing across the horizon. I ignite into flames as I head closer and closer to the sun until I am fully engulfed in fire. I fly high, dip down, and dance in the Asphodel air—the legendary beast rising from the blazes of Hell. Free from the confines of not only time and space but also form and spirit.

I crash back to the ground in front of Malek and cover my body in my burning wings. The entire world shakes and trembles at my descent. As I rise, burnt feathers fall to a heap at my feet, and I transform back to my human-like self. Malek is awe-struck. His eyes are open wide and his mouth slightly slack-jawed.

I raise an eyebrow. "Like that?" I ask.

It takes him a second to get his words organized. "Yes," he answers, breathing out. "I'd say definitely like that."

"But I don't belong here, Malek. I can feel it. Asphodel is not my place. Just like I felt it when I returned to Ilarium, it didn't feel right. Asphodel cannot hold me if that makes any sense."

"Yes," he says. "I understand. You are much larger now than the limitations of Asphodel. We must go to him right away."

"Lucifer?"

Malek huffs a little chuckle. "Who else?" And he outspreads his black wings. "We don't have these for nothing, ya know. Come on."

I imitate his actions, and he takes off ahead of me. I follow closely behind as he leads me flying across the fog world of Asphodel to a wide, rocky crater that descends deep below the surface of the world. We hover over the precipice of the depression as wind gusts bob us up and down. Malek points to the deepness of the cave and begins to slowly descend, and I nod and follow, gliding gracefully into the spiky mouth of the basin.

On my descent, the sounds of screams and moans fill the rocky cave. Wraiths screech past us every now and then, and when we arrive at the bottom, hordes of ghouls and distorted beasts swarm the opening of a tunnel.

"This is where my father lives. This is Gehenna," Malek says as he lands swiftly next to me.

The monsters cry out in pain and agony. "What are they?" I ask.

"Souls of the damned. The throwaways. The leftovers."

A feeling of shock comes over me. "Dead? Dead human souls?"

Malek nods.

I shake my head in disbelief. "That's not possible. When a soul passes on they are either made an Ishim in Ilarium or are reabsorbed into the breath of the Creator. Human souls have no place in Gehenna, the Land of Punishment. Human souls aren't to be damned, or punished, or..."

"Punished?" He turns his mouth up to question me. "Oh, no! Aestrangel! They're not being punished! This is their pleasure! This is their paradise. They have taken on the shape and form of their deepest desires and will live for eternity in their own personal heaven. Do you really think your maker would reabsorb the souls of the truly wicked? Not so, Morning Glory. They are given up to Lucifer."

More lies. More lies to keep us in the dark and in line.

Malek guides me through the tunnel and the moans and sounds of lamentation gets louder. At each turn, we pass alcoves where creatures hang upside down on crosses while demons lash metal-studded whips against their naked flesh. Pools of blood cover the stony floor, and as I look to each one moaning and writhing in terror, I begin to understand the torments are not unwelcomed. The torture is wanted and desired, and the faces of the creatures in these scenes of brutality are smiling. They are smiling.

We reach the throne room, and I enter with the greatest amount of reverence and caution I can muster. The pungent scent of flowers overcomes my senses, and Lucifer rises from his chair to greet me. He is ageless with pale skin and dark features, as he appears to me in the shape of a man—something familiar and recognizable to my mind. *I remember you*, I think. *I remember the grace of your body, your cold, icy touch, and your beguiling black eyes.* He wears a long black robe, and the aura that flickers along the outline of his stately posture pulsates the most curious shades of blacks and grays—the colors of death and

despair and depression and reckless abandon: the fragments of black lightning from when he fell from Ilarium. And just as I remember from our first meeting, I am completely and utterly drawn to his hypnotic aura.

"Once again, I welcome you back," he says with a deep, melodic voice. He flashes me a perfectly white-toothed smile, glides over, and stretches out his arms.

Quickly, I find myself not hesitating, and I embrace the Dark Lord, fall into his open arms as he runs his hands up and down my back and wings. His power ripples over my skin in waves of throbbing ecstasy. It rolls throughout my body, deep into the muscles of my being, in the depths of my chest, and pours out of the tips of my feathers. I close my eyes from the pleasurable sensation and nestle my head on top of his shoulder. I don't want him to end this touch, this feeling, this hypnotizing embrace, but I'm not sure if I can handle the extreme feeling of pleasure any longer. Without warning, he eases his grip on me, and I relax.

Before I break our hold, I open my eyes and look around the throne room. Off to the side, in a shadowy corner, a woman-figure lies dreamily on a black, canopied bed. I must squint my eyes to make sure she is there and not just a figment of my imagination. She is staring at me with narrowed eyes, and I can sense she is darting anger and jealousy in my direction. When she moves on the bed, her long black hair tumbles over her face, and the lower part of her body writhes with the rhythm of a giant snake. Slowly, I pull away from Lucifer, and take a step to the side, observing the lovely creature.

"Oh, child," Lucifer says, "that is Lilith. You didn't have the pleasure of making her acquaintance the last time you were here."

I bow my head respectfully in her direction, but she slithers off the bed and across the rocky floor and through a doorway to another room in the abode.

"You have done well," he says to me, and he speaks in the language of the humans—hundreds of languages simultaneously. His voice is commanding and dark and echoes off the rock walls and bounces off the corners of my head.

"Well?" I ask. "How so? I failed your Calling!"

Laughter escapes Lucifer's mouth. Deep and resonating. His long black hair falls forward as his entire body is rocked with mirth. I look over to Malek standing behind me, and he, too, looks a bit perplexed. Perhaps he has never seen his father in such a state before.

"Aestrangel!" he exclaims as he begins to calm down. "You didn't fail! You did exactly as I wanted." He claps his hands together like a child who has miraculously solved a grand mystery. "The humans, the mission, the Calling. Malek was a good guide, but he never had anything important to offer to the situation. There was nothing he could have done that you weren't completely capable of doing yourself. That was all secondary to the real task at hand. I knew you wouldn't be able to go through with it, with convincing that human girl to take the life of her loved one. In fact, I didn't want you to do that."

My ears hear his words, and yet I am taking too long to process them because I get a little confused. By the look on Malek's face, he is confused as well.

"I... I don't understand," I stammer. "Was all that for *nothing*?"

The Morning Star puts his arm around me lovingly, like a father does when explaining something to their child. I am embraced not only by his touch but also by his icy aura that encompasses my whole body like a white snake curling its tail around my soul. "No, Aestrangel. Absolutely not. What you gained from your time on Earth was priceless. Invaluable. You learned things about human nature and the human condition you could not have learned had you not been there. You need to be able to serve them well, and without that knowledge, you would have been an ineffective ruler."

I pause and pull back at his words.

"You also learned things about yourself," he continues. "Things you never fully realized in your angel form. You learned your true nature and have just begun exploring the depths of your capabilities. You have learned to hone your emotions and to let them propel you to great lengths. And when you sacrificed yourself, it was a brilliant move. Because when you went back to your precious Ilarium, it was only a matter of time before the pact we made would be broken. I have no power in that realm, and the memories you asked me to erase were bound to come back to you. And when they did! And what you did! You did something no one could have done, not even me. You killed Camael. He no longer exists. I have been waiting eons for an opportunity like that. I have been biding my time for the moment of truth for my good ole adversary." He strokes a strand of hair away from my eyes. The motion of his fingers against my brow is magnetic. "And so," he

continues as he leads me to a chair next to his black crystal throne, "you have done something for me I could have never done myself. You were chosen, from the beginning of time, for greatness. And you have proven to be my most valued ally for avenging the punishment of Lilith, and the millions of my legion from the beginning of our time." He motions for me to sit in the chair. It is smaller, and less decorative than his seat, but it is grand all the same.

So I was just a pawn in Lucifer's plan too?

I feel sick. I sit in the elaborate chair, but my stomach feels achy and weak like I'm going to throw up all over the stone floor. I feel dirty and violated and used. They *all* used me! Every one of them! They all had some stupid plan and somehow, someway, I just happened to fit into their predicaments. Lies. Betrayal. Deception. A world I believed to be clearly black and white no longer has a clear definition. All parties involved in my grand manipulation are disgusting creatures! All parties involved in my ultimate betrayal will have to suffer the consequences!

"You shall sit at my right-hand side," Lucifer continues, and I bite back my rage, "and be General in our ongoing battle for the pursuit of the ultimate throne."

Malek is frozen in place. Speechless. Awe-stuck. Confused. Hurt. And a little bit jealous. I can read him so easily now as he wears his emotions on the front of his face. I can tell he had no knowledge of any of this, and in a way, I feel badly for him because he looks to his father now with an expression of betrayal as well.

Lucifer produces a crown made of black thorns and places it atop my head, digging it deeply into my scalp so it will remain there forever. I wince at first but maintain my composure. Droplets of blood trickle down my forehead and temples.

I stare at Malek who cringes too when the crown is presented to me, and my heart feels heavy for him. He now knows what it feels like to be used by those you love the most.

Lucifer adjusts the crown a little and sits at his throne—pleased with me, pleased with himself. "You have yet to reach your full power and potential, Aestrangel. I have seen what you have done—how you massacred an entire human bloodline and how you used your unbridled strength to eliminate one of the highest-ranking angels. The world has no idea what they are in for. Now more than ever, they will shudder under your black wings."

Malek's shoulders slump forward, and he exhales loudly. The fierce storm in his eyes is gone, left now with a vacancy that scares me. He tugs nervously at his medallion and opens his mouth to say something to The Morning Star—*his father*, the one he always listened to and obeyed—but Lucifer waves his hand in the air, dismissing his own son. Malek gives me one last pained look, turns on his heels, and glides out of the throne room and back into the rocky corridor.

I look at Lucifer from the corner of my eye with disdain. He is poised. Relaxed. Sure of himself. And his arrogance only fuels my anger even more.

And I can't help but think:

Oh yes, Malek. The world will shudder under my black wings.
And so will The Morning Star.

BOOK CLUB QUESTIONS

1. How does the information presented in the prologue shape how you feel about Aestrangel?

2. How has the relationship between Aestrangel and Malek changed? How do you feel about their interactions?

3. Revalia and Lozhure return in order to prevent Aestrangel from completing her mission, but do you think they have good intentions? What is their role in the way things play out? Are they a detriment? Do they propel Aestrangel's desire to help Lucifer?

4. Discuss the symbolism of the snakes in the desert. Discuss the symbolism of the angels in the desert.

5. Do you think Aestrangel really wants to manipulate people? Knowing what you know about her and how she once valued humanity, do you think she truly has ill intentions?

6. How does Malek feel about Aestrangel? With her growing power, will this cause a rift in their relationship?

7. The Judges in Ilarium—Och, Oethra, and Razelle, give Aestra a cryptic message when they say "He's chosen you, Aestra." What do you think is the double meaning behind this?

8. When Aestra is reunited with Camael, it does not end well. Why do you think she reacted in such an extreme way? What do you think the ultimate consequences of those actions will be?

9. By the end, Aestrangel has committed herself to overthrowing Lucifer. What conflict do you think that will present for Malek?

10. You've finished the book. Now go back and re-read the prologue in the context of an epilogue. Have your feelings/thoughts/perceptions changed about Aestrangel?

Author Bio

Maria DeVivo writes horror and dark fantasy for both a YA and an adult audience. Each of her series has been Amazon bestsellers and has won multiple awards since 2012. When not writing, she teaches Language Arts and Journalism to middle school students in Florida. A lover of all things dark and demented, the worlds she creates are fantastical and immersive. Get swept away in the lands of elves, zombies, angels, demons, and witches (but not all in the same place). Maria takes great pleasure in warping the comfort factor in her readers' minds—just when you think you've reached a safe space in her stories, she snaps you back into her twisted reality.

MORE BOOKS FROM
4 HORSEMEN PUBLICATIONS

PARANORMAL & URBAN FANTASY

AMANDA FASCIANO
Waking Up Dead
Dead Vessel
Dead Show
Dead Revelations

BEAU LAKE
The Beast Beside Me
The Beast Within Me
Taming the Beast: Novella
The Beast After Me
Charming the Beast
The Beast Like Me
An Eye for Emeralds
Swimming in Sapphires
Pining for Pearls

CHELSEA BURTON DUNN
By Moonlight
Moon Bound

J.M. PAQUETTE
Call Me Forth
Invite Me In
Keep Me Close

KAIT DISNEY-LEUGERS
Antique Magic
Blood Magic
Heart Magic

LYRA R. SAENZ
Prelude
Falsetto in the Woods: Novella
Ragtime Swing

Sonata
Song of the Sea
The Devil's Trill
Bercuese
To Heal a Songbird
Ghost March
Nocturne

MARIA DEVIVO
Aestrangel the Fallen
Aestrangel the Chosen
Aestrangel the Risen

MEGAN MACKIE
The Saint of Liars
The Devil's Day
The Finder of the Lucky Devil

PAIGE LAVOIE
I'm in Love with Mothman
I'm Engaged to Mothman

ROBERT J. LEWIS
Shadow Guardian and the Three Bears
Shadow Guardian and the Big Bad Wolf
Shadow Guardian and the Boys
That Went Woof

VALERIE WILLIS
Cedric: The Demonic Knight
Romasanta: Father of Werewolves
The Oracle: Keeper of the Gaea's Gate
Artemis: Eye of Gaea
King Incubus: A New Reign

FANTASY

D. LAMBERT
To Walk into the Sands
Rydan
Celebrant
Northlander
Esparan
King
Traitor
His Last Name

D.A. SPRUZEN
The Turkish Connection
The Witch of Tut

DANIELLE ORSINO
Locked Out of Heaven
Thine Eyes of Mercy
From the Ashes
Kingdom Come
Fire, Ice, Acid, & Heart
A Fae is Done

J.M. PAQUETTE
Klauden's Ring
Solyn's Body
The Inbetween
Hannah's Heart

LOU KEMP
The Violins Played Before Junstan
Music Shall Untune the Sky
The Raven and the Pig
The Pirate Danced and the Automat Died
The Wyvern, the Pirate, and the Madman

MEGAN MACKIE
Silverblood Scion

R.J. YOUNG
Challenges of Tawa
Witch of the Whirlwind

SYDNEY WILDER
Daughter of Serpents

VALERIE WILLIS
Cedric: The Demonic Knight
Romasanta: Father of Werewolves
The Oracle: Keeper of the Gaea's Gate
Artemis: Eye of Gaea
King Incubus: A New Reign

KYLE SORRELL
Munderworld
Potarium

DISCOVER MORE AT
4HORSEMENPUBLICATIONS.COM